Silver Serpent, Golden Sword

~ Tales of Karensa ~

Jean Cullop

Scripture Union

By the same author

Tales of Karensa: Where Dolphins race with Rainbows
Tales of Karensa: Castle of Shadows
Tales of Karensa: Children of the Second Morning

Copyright © Jean Cullop
First published 2002
Reprinted 2002

Scripture Union, 207–209 Queensway, Bletchley,
Milton Keynes, MK2 2EB, England.
Email: info@scriptureunion.org.uk
Website: www.scriptureunion.org.uk

ISBN 1 85999 555 1

All rights reserved. No part of this publication may be
reproduced, stored in a retrieval system, or transmitted in
any form or by any means, electronic, mechanical,
photocopying, recording or otherwise, without the prior
permission of Scripture Union.

The right of Jean Cullop to be identified as author of this
work has been asserted by her in accordance with the
Copyright, Designs and Patents Act 1988.

British Library Cataloguing-in-Publication Data.
A catalogue record of this book is available from the British
Library.

Printed and bound in Great Britain by Creative Print and
Design (Wales) Ebbw Vale.

Scripture Union is an international Christian charity working
with churches in more than 130 countries, providing
resources to bring the good news about Jesus Christ to
children, young people and families and to encourage them
to develop spiritually through the Bible and prayer.

As well as our network of volunteers, staff and associates
who run holidays, church-based events and school Christian
groups, we produce a wide range of publications and
support those who use our resources through training
programmes.

Contents

To Holly

Fisher village

Harbour

Farmland

Petroc's farm

High Hill

road

Dark Forest

Narrow track

Black Rock Bay

road

Carrik's house

Farmland

Fields

coastal path

King's Palace

Dark Forest

Bellum's Castle

Stream

Ford

Kett's house

Meadow of Flowers

Bay of Dolphins

Moors

The far side of the island

Farms

Jay's Barn

Reuben's house

Town

Farms

Bay of Perils

Karensa

The Lost Kingdom

As far away as yesterday is an island called Karensa, where dolphins race with rainbows and woodland creatures walk freely in the Dark Forest, and broken hearts are healed.

The people of Karensa lived and spoke in ways unchanging since ancient times and each one could go to the King, who met every need with perfect love and justice.

Then came the Day of Sorrow when Lord Bellum disobeyed the King and for that he was cast from the Royal Palace. Fear was born on Karensa, and the way to the King was closed.

Lord Bellum built his own castle, for he was determined that one day he, not the King, would be ruler of Karensa, and many people believed the false promises he made.

The King's word decreed that the punishment for disobedience was death, and the King would not put his own desires above the truth of his word. His people must die.

Yet this King loved his people more than they would ever know, and in love sent his son, Salvis, to die in their place, although his own heart was broken.

So it was at the very moment Salvis died, all those who were held captive in Bellum's castle were set free and defeat was turned into a great victory.

Salvis now lives again in the Royal Palace and all who put their trust in him are forgiven and receive the King's power. Once again they may approach the King, who even from the silence of their hearts, will hear them.

So it will be on Karensa until the day that Salvis rides out from the Palace and claims back the Lost Kingdom.

Meanwhile, on the far side of the island, a new government has been established called the Guardians, who meet every need of each person, yet who will not accept Salvis or the King, and who oppose those who remain loyal to the truth.

The Decision

Time races towards a New Tomorrow,
Familiar days become uncertain night,
And some despair, for they grow weary
In the long, eternal fight.

Which will you choose to follow
When the battle scenes unfold?
The serpent cast in silver,
Or the two-edged sword of gold?

Chapter 1

Black Rock Bay

Petroc watched two dolphins playing in the sea, rainbows of light cascading from the water as their sleek, grey bodies leapt through the waves.

"Telki! Praze!" he called, but they were too far away to hear him, and swam off to deeper water. They made Petroc think of Luke and Rosie, his friends who had once been guided to Karensa by these dolphins.

He threw a cloak over his woollen tunic. He was cold. The season called the Time of Plenty was late this year. Trees were still bright with blossom, and in the fields the corn was growing slowly.

From High Hill it was possible to see most of the island. Below him was the farm where he now lived with his mother, his sister, Morwen and his Uncle Amos who had helped them since Petroc's father died.

Beyond the farm was the Dark Forest and the golden turrets of the Royal Palace. Further away stood the castle of the King's enemy, Lord Bellum. Petroc always shivered when he saw that dark stronghold where he was once imprisoned. Lord Bellum's followers increased daily as the dark-haired lord slowly gained control of the island. Petroc and his family were loyal to the King, which meant that they were now disliked by many people on Karensa.

In the opposite direction was the coast, and there, as always, mist obscured the horizon. He could see Black Rock Bay and smaller, sandy coves leading to the great Bay of Dolphins in the far distance.

Quite suddenly, and without warning, a thought came to him: Go to Black Rock Bay.

Petroc shook his head in disbelief. Morwen said that sometimes the King's son, Salvis, spoke thoughts into her heart, but this didn't happen to Petroc. Was the thought really from Salvis, or just his own imagination? Black Rock Bay was dangerous. Why would Salvis want him to go there?

Go to Black Rock Bay, the thought insisted.

He decided to go. If it was only his imagination, he had nothing to lose. It was too cold to sit here any longer. If the thought really had come from Salvis, he should obey.

He stood up, brushed his tunic and trousers, removed grass from his hair and pulled his cloak around his shoulders.

In Cornwall, summer was late this year. This was the first day of the school holidays, yet the sky was still grey and the air cool. Soon, many visitors would arrive, but it seemed unlikely that they would find the sun.

Luke and Rosie walked across Poldawn Cove. Usually, they would be accompanied by their dog, Pepper, but today, Dad and his wife, Stacey, had taken Pepper to the vet for her vaccinations. The young people missed the little border collie dancing around them, barking at the waves.

"This is the last time we'll have the beach to ourselves for the next six weeks," Luke grumbled. He flung a pebble as far as he could into the surf.

Rosie copied him, but being nearly three years younger than her brother, she couldn't throw as far.

"I like the visitors," she replied. "I know the shops are crowded and the beach isn't our own any more, but I like it when they arrive. It's as if... as if we're showing them our home. Sharing it with them."

Luke didn't agree. To him, crowded streets were a nuisance. He conveniently forgot that many of their neighbours owned hotels, cafés and shops.

He pulled the hood of his jacket over his fair hair and said, as if proving a point, "Now it's raining!"

"Come on," his sister replied, "let's shelter in the cave! It's only a shower!"

They raced across the sand, Rosie's face stinging as the wind blew strands of her long, fair hair across her cheeks. From the cave they watched the rain sweep across the bay. Rosie found a scrunchie in the pocket of her jeans and tied back her wet hair.

"You can't see the horizon any more," she observed. "It reminds me of the island."

Luke remained silent.

"D'you ever want to go back there?" she persisted.

"To Karensa? I don't know. Sometimes I do, just a bit."

Karensa was a strange island which they had now visited twice, where they had met the wonderful Lord Salvis and where they had learnt so much

11

about themselves. On this island their lives had been changed for ever. The very mention of Karensa reminded them of what was important and what didn't really matter.

Luke sighed. "On Karensa, right was right, and wrong was wrong. Here..."

"Here it's different," Rosie agreed. "Dad and Stacey tell us one thing, teachers tell us something else and then in church, people say we should share our faith. When we do share, we're laughed at."

"Not always. One or two of my friends have come to church. One even came back a second time."

"Rachel?"

"Yes... She might come again."

Rosie knew that Rachel's interest was in Luke, not in church, but she didn't say so. Luke played in the school rugby team and Rachel had accepted a dare to go out with every boy in the team.

There was no point in discouraging Luke. She changed the subject.

"At least on Karensa there were no exams! There wasn't even school!"

Luke was still being serious. "I'd like to see Petroc and Morwen."

"So would I," Rosie agreed. "And Salvis. Oh, I should love to be near Salvis again! Sometimes I want to see him so much it hurts."

The rain didn't stop. Luke peered into the cave behind them.

"We've never explored this cave, Rosie. Let's see how far back it goes."

"It might be dangerous. We have to watch the tides," Rosie objected weakly.

She knew that she was wasting her breath. Some things about Luke never changed. When he made up his mind to do something, it was useless to argue. Rosie followed him.

The cave was long and narrow, eroded by rough seas, and as they crept further into the darkness, they could only just see each other. It was very wet. Slimy seaweed dripped from the walls. The sand moved beneath their feet which meant that there was water below the surface.

"The sea comes right in," Rosie said nervously.

"But the tide's on the turn," Luke pointed out. "Hey, look, Rosie, there's daylight ahead. This cave must come out on the next beach. Watch yourself here, the roof gets a bit low. Mind you don't bang your head. Bend down."

Rosie obeyed. They half walked, half crawled, until suddenly they could stand upright once more and were looking at a rocky cove.

"Oh, wicked!" Luke exclaimed. "I never knew this was here!"

"It's stopped raining, too," said Rosie. "Let's explore!"

They were standing on a shingle beach which was scattered with dark rocks. Luke ran his fingers through his hair as he often did when he was puzzled.

"That's strange," he muttered. "We've never been here before, yet it seems familiar..."

Rosie didn't hear him. She was having a great time, jumping from rock to rock across the beach. Seeing her do this, Luke was reminded of another day, so long ago.

"Black Rock Bay!" he breathed. "But it... it can't—"

Before he could finish speaking, Rosie raced back.

"The sea's coming in, Luke! It's coming up the beach, fast! We'll be cut off by the tide! We must go back!"

"Yes, we must," he muttered. "If we don't go back now, it will be too late. Come on!"

They ran deep into the cave, looking for the tunnel.

"I can't find the way!" Luke's voice rose in panic as the sea splashed his feet.

"It must be here! The tunnel can't have disappeared!"

They searched desperately, but they found only a solid wall. The sea seeped through their trainers.

Rosie was really scared now. "Luke, what shall we do? We've got to get out of here! What shall we do?"

"I don't know!" he shouted.

Luke grabbed Rosie's hand and pulled her outside. When he saw the sea crashing wildly around them, he was scared, too.

He tried to keep calm. If they really were in Black Rock Bay there should be a cliff path, but it was steep and treacherous. His eyes scanned the cliffs. Sure enough, the path was there, but it looked even more dangerous than he remembered as the wild sea crashed over it.

Rosie looked at the way they must go. Her dismay was obvious. "Oh, I don't like heights!"

"Then you'd better learn to like them," he told her grimly. "Either that, or drown." Then, because she was his young sister and because they had shared so many dangers together, he added, "Rosie, you know you can do it. You're as brave as anyone else. You go first. I'll be behind. If you slip, I'll be there."

Rosie looked up to the steep cliff, then back to the sea, swirling angrily around their feet and rapidly getting deeper. She had no choice.

Taking a deep breath, she pulled herself up the path, her hands clinging tightly to the rock face.

With Luke shouting encouragement, she did her best, but the path was slippery and she was very scared. When they had nearly reached the top, fear overtook her. She hesitated.

"Don't look down!" her brother yelled. "Go on, Rosie, you're doing well. We're nearly there!"

Rosie closed her eyes. She was dizzy. A huge wave crashed, far below them. She lost her grip on the rock and felt herself falling backwards.

Luke was unable to help her, for she was falling away from him, out of his reach. As she fell, it was like watching a video played in slow motion.

"Take hold of me!" a voice shouted from above them. Hands caught Rosie's hands and held them tightly. Her arms felt as though they were being wrenched from their sockets as she was hauled upwards.

Luke followed her, slipping and scrambling, grazing his knuckles on the sharp rocks, until the strong hands caught him, too, and pulled him over the cliff edge to safety.

They lay in the long, dry grass, eyes closed, frightened and exhausted.

After a little while, Rosie sat up, curious to see

who had rescued her. She looked into a pair of green eyes that she remembered so well.

"Petroc? It can't be! What are you doing here? How did you get to Cornwall?"

Luke sat up too. He was strangely calm, as if he was being carried along by a mighty plan that was not of his own making.

The two boys stared at each other.

"Hello, Petroc," Luke said shakily. "We're not in Cornwall, are we? This is Karensa."

Chapter 2

"Brothers then and brothers now"

Rosie stared at the cove below them and the mist beyond. "That must be Black Rock Bay! There's the hill where we used to pick blackberries! I remember!" She turned around. "The Dark Forest! We really are on Karensa!"

"You wanted to come back, and now we're here," said Luke.

"I said I missed Salvis. I never said I wanted to come back to the island!" Rosie protested.

"You did! That's exactly what you said!"

They did not seem very happy to be back. Petroc felt uncomfortable. "Aren't you pleased to see me?"

"Of course we are," Rosie muttered. "It's just that we... we didn't expect to come back, that's all. It's a bit of a shock." Then, as she looked at the tall, red-headed boy, her heart skipped a beat. She had always liked Petroc. When they had first met, she had only been nine. Now she was older and her feelings towards him were quite different. "Of course we're pleased to see you, Petroc. We just have to get used to being back on Karensa."

There was an awkward silence.

"How are Morwen, and your mother?" asked Luke politely.

"They are well. Morwen grows more lovely each

day. Mother is frail. The years have overtaken her."

It was strange to hear the island way of speaking again.

Rosie pulled herself to her feet. She was trembling.

"It's cold. My jeans are wet. Can we dry off somewhere? Can we go to the farm, Petroc?"

Petroc stood up. He was taller than Rosie had remembered; much taller than Luke.

"Where else would you go? My home is your home, you know that. Come." He pulled Luke to his feet. Once they had been like brothers. Now they seemed more like strangers, not knowing what to say to each other.

"I didn't thank you, Petroc," said Rosie. "I believe you saved my life. I might easily have dragged you over the cliff with me when you caught me."

He shrugged. "You were a sister to me. You still are."

Luke and Rosie followed Petroc as they turned from the coastal path and skirted the Dark Forest. People said that when you returned to a place, it seemed smaller than you remembered, yet this was not so. The forest was as dark as ever. Above them and far away, they knew that the turrets of the Royal Palace gleamed, and beyond the Palace stood the stronghold of Lord Bellum.

"Nothing has changed!" Luke exclaimed.

"Oh yes it has, Luke." Petroc's voice sounded sad. "Karensa is not the same. More and more people have joined Lord Bellum. The King's people are not popular any more. Our homes have been attacked. Crops have been spoilt. Some of our friends have been beaten and robbed."

"It sounds like home," Luke observed dryly.

"Where you live?"

"Our world is like that all the time."

"Why?"

"No reason. It's just the way things are—"

"Ssh!" Petroc stopped, suddenly wary. He pointed to the Dark Forest. A rider on a grey horse was watching them.

The horseman lifted his hand and beckoned. He looked familiar, but he was too far away for them to see his face. Rosie wondered if it was Salvis, but she didn't think so. "Perhaps he wants us to follow him," she said.

Petroc was unsure. "I don't know if we should. We cannot trust folk as we once did."

"If we stay together we'll be safe," she reasoned. "There are three of us. We've faced worse danger in the past."

Petroc was nervous, but he wasn't going to admit it, so they turned from their way to follow the horseman, who led them deep into the Dark Forest.

Luke breathed the pine-scented air of the forest and it brought back many memories, some happy, some sad. A big part of him wished he had never gone into that cave in Poldawn. He was now happy in Cornwall and had many friends. They had made plans for the school holidays, so how long would he and Rosie stay here this time? Time was different on Karensa, and the holidays would still be waiting for them when they got home, but Luke was not sure he wanted to turn aside from his plans, even for a little while.

Rosie was quiet. For a brief moment she had longed to return to the island, and already she was aware that they were near to Salvis, but did she really want to stay here?

Petroc was deep in thought. Many times he had imagined Luke and Rosie returning, but now they were here, it felt strange. Also, he was uneasy about going so far into the Dark Forest where they could easily be attacked.

As they came to a ford across a river, the rider was suddenly gone. They looked around, puzzled. They were alone, and, Luke believed, lost.

Before he could say anything, Petroc disappeared. One minute he was there, the next he was gone.

Luke glared at his sister. "Now look what you've done!"

"Me? I didn't do anything!" She took a step back from him, then she vanished, too.

He scratched his head, bewildered and more and more annoyed. This was no time to play games.

He turned to see where his sister had gone, and at once he started to fall backwards until he landed on a bed of soft, dry ferns.

Luke sat up. He was in a cave, created from overhanging bushes and trees and surrounded by thick foliage. Petroc and Rosie were laughing at him. He forgot to be annoyed and laughed with them.

But his laughter froze, as bitter sweet memories flooded his heart.

"I know this place. The ford... the cave... I ... I've been here before... I think..."

He shifted his collar to one side, revealing a long white scar on his shoulder.

"You described a place like this the day you got that scar," she said gently, aware that he was deeply hurt about what happened that day.

Petroc and Luke stared at each other. It was in this very woodland cave that Petroc had once sacrificed his own freedom to protect his friend. Luke's shoulder had been ripped open by a sharp branch and Petroc had given himself up to save him from being captured. That night, alone in a blizzard, blood oozing from his shoulder, Luke would have died if Salvis had not come to rescue him.*

The barriers crumbled and crashed.

"Oh Luke, I have missed you so much!" Petroc cried. "Every day I have thought of you and Rosie!"

"I've missed you too," Luke admitted.

"We are still brothers, then?"

"Brothers then and brothers now. I never forgot you, Petroc, nor the island."

"Is it good that you are back?"

Luke had a lump in his throat. Why was it so easy to cry on Karensa? He thought he knew the answer; it was because they were so close to Salvis. The King's son had the power to touch hearts and stir deep emotions.

"It is good that we are back, my brother," he replied, speaking in the way of the island people. The two boys clasped hands in fellowship.

Rosie was beginning to feel forgotten, but before

---

*This story is told in *Where Dolphins Race with Rainbows*.

she could say so, they were startled to see a face peeping through the foliage above them. The face was thin, and sharp-featured beneath tangled fair hair.

Petroc's mouth fell open with surprise. "Esram! What are you doing here?"

Before the face could reply, another joined it, a girl with plain features and straight, mouse-coloured hair. Luke and Rosie shouted together.

"Holly!"

The last time Luke and Rosie had visited Karensa they had stayed on the far side of the island, and that was where they had met Holly and Esram. Holly's father, Reuben, had taken them into his home.*

Petroc knew Esram, who, with his Uncle Carrik, had been Petroc's enemy until they had both decided to serve the King. Now they were on the far side of the island, telling people what Salvis had done for them.

When the excitement of meeting each other again was over, Esram explained why they were here and introduced Holly to Petroc.

"Things are much worse on the far side of the island," he said. "The Guardians are still in control and things are very hard for the King's followers. Some are in prison, just for their loyalty to the King. Any who dare speak against the Guardians are considered enemies. It is no longer safe to talk openly about Salvis or the King. Reuben and Carrik are in hiding on the High Moors in fear of

---

*This story is told in *Children of the Second Morning*.

22

their freedom and even their lives. They have sent us here to safety."

Luke and Rosie exchanged glances. The people on the far side of the island had always been well cared for and healthy, but Esram and Holly were thin and pale. The journey from the High Moors would not account for this change.

Petroc made a wry face. "It is becoming difficult here, too. It would only take one strong leader to make our lives very hard."

"We are not liked or accepted," Holly said sadly. "Yet we know that Salvis is wonderful and we want to share this with people who don't know him."

"It's a bit like that in our world," said Rosie. "If we try to tell our friends about the Great King, we're laughed at, sometimes even bullied."

The young people were silent.

"It's not easy serving the Great King," said Luke at last.

They were interrupted by the sound of approaching horses, and from their hiding place they watched a troop of soldiers, coming from the direction of the far side of the island; soldiers dressed in dark grey with cloaks of midnight blue. Each man carried the emblem of a silver serpent on his tunic and shield.

Their leader was a handsome man with hair the colour of ripe corn, and behind him rode a girl of about fourteen, a very pretty girl with thick, brown hair, huge dark eyes and a pale olive skin. She was dressed in a tunic of dark gold silk and her trousers and cloak were of velvet.

Hardly daring to breathe, they watched the troop

ford the river, the horses splashing the clear, cold water.

When they had gone, Holly dropped to her knees, covering her face with her hands.

"Oh, I cannot believe this! Petroc, that man with yellow hair is Tomas, the leader of the Guardians, and the girl is Lindis, his daughter. We have travelled these many miles to escape them, but the Guardians have followed us here!"

Chapter 3

Silver serpent, golden sword

"The Guardians cannot be here!" Esram exclaimed in dismay.

"Why have they come?" asked Rosie.

"They mean to rule here, just like they do at home. You are slow, Rosie," Holly told her.

Rosie wasn't too hurt by her remark. Holly was bossy but she didn't mean all she said. It was just her way.

"If the people here love the King," Luke reasoned, "surely they won't welcome the Guardians?"

Esram laughed bitterly. "Oh, they will welcome them! You will see. When families are hungry and the Guardians give them food, they will welcome them!"

"If they help people, they cannot be so bad, then?" asked Petroc.

"Very bad," Holly replied firmly. "That is how they gain control. They give away things like food and medicine. They win people's trust. Then they take away their freedom by making them obey their laws."

Rosie was trying to make sense of this. She nudged her brother. "Luke, we always come here for a reason," she whispered. "Maybe this is the reason... Petroc, maybe we are here to help you?"

"Maybe," he said, in a very tired voice. Petroc

grew weary in the struggle. After Lord Bellum's men had destroyed his farm, it had been rebuilt and was flourishing again. Crops were in the fields. Trees in the orchard would soon be laden with fruit. Not one single lamb had been lost this year. Petroc was enjoying life again after so many bad things had happened to him. Now his happiness was about to be spoilt. Serving the King was an endless battle.

He pulled himself to his feet. "We should go back to the farm," he sighed wearily.

The others moved to follow him, but as they did so, the rider on the grey horse re-appeared from a nearby thicket.

"It's Lord Veritan!" Rosie cried.

Veritan rode up to them and dismounted. He was awesome, almost a giant! The circlet he wore over his long, silver hair sparkled with priceless jewels, as did his belt of silver and the hilt of his great sword.

Holly whispered, "Who is he? He's so big!" She had never seen Veritan before and was just a little afraid.

No-one answered, so, like the others, she bowed her head before the Lord of the Palace. They would have knelt, but Veritan himself had once told them that they should only kneel before the King or Salvis.

"I am Veritan, the King's messenger," he told her. "You need not fear. The King has sent me to you, to bring you together and then to speak with you."

"Did you bring us back to Karensa?" Rosie asked.

Veritan smiled. "Not me, child. Your own desire to return brought you back here. And Luke, it was your desire too. Do not lay the responsibility upon your sister."

Luke grinned sheepishly.

"Petroc, son of Tobias," Lord Veritan continued, "your family's loyalty has been noticed by the King. I have a message for you this day."

"What is that, Lord?" Petroc knew that Veritan would only bring good things to them.

Veritan lifted up his great sword for them all to see.

"This is the golden sword of truth, which can never be defeated. I am here to prepare you for a great battle. The Guardians are here to stay, and Tomas, their leader, serves Lord Bellum. This sword represents the King's word, the true law that is written in the hearts of all those who belong to him. Bellum and the Guardians have taken a silver serpent as their emblem, but that serpent will never overcome the golden sword. Now, you must all kneel."

No-one spoke. The young people sensed that something very special was about to happen.

Then Luke was heard to mutter, "He told us not to kneel to him before," but no-one took any notice, and he felt foolish.

As they knelt in this place that meant so much to Luke and Petroc, the woodland became strangely silent. No creature stirred; no deer or squirrel, rabbit or bird. The Dark Forest sensed the awesome nearness of its mighty Creator.

"I do this with the King's authority," Veritan told them, in a very serious voice. "You must keep perfectly still. I shall use the sword of truth to empower each of you, but the golden sword is only a tool. Never forget, the power will come from the King, not the sword."

He rested the two-edged blade of the golden sword on each of their heads in turn. The light of day deepened to that of a glorious sunset as he asked the King to strengthen them.

When it was done, and daylight returned, Petroc asked, "Lord, what of my sister? She is not here."

"When you return home, you and Esram should place your hands on Morwen and ask the King to give to her that which you have received. As you ask, so shall it be done."

Then Veritan spoke even more seriously. "The truth of the King's word will be your protection. Some of you," he looked directly at Petroc, "will be called to suffer for your loyalty to the King. Always obey the King. Do not ever forsake that which you know to be pure and true. Now go, all of you. If you take the small track to your left, you will reach the cliff path and soon be home."

As he watched them walk away, Veritan stroked his waiting horse. He spoke softly and sadly.

"May the King protect them and make them strong. They will need that strength in the days ahead."

The Royal Palace was the living heart of Karensa from where the King ruled with his son, Salvis, and the Unseen Lord. Their mighty presence illuminated the Palace with silver, gold and rose, the lights continually moving and changing.

Lord Veritan knelt before the Three Thrones.

"Is it accomplished?" asked the King in a voice at once mighty and just.

"Yes, Lord King. I have done everything you asked of me."

Salvis leant forward. He was no longer the simple peasant the children had known in the Bay of Dolphins. His clothes were dazzling white and he wore a wonderful crown of moving light. His face was brighter than the sun, and his eyes blazed with incredible love.

When Salvis spoke, his voice was strong and powerful, yet gentle and compassionate.

"The time is coming when I shall ride from the Royal Palace and defeat Bellum for ever. Until then, Father, I will continue to plead day and night for your people. It is your will that all shall turn back to you so that each person may live with us in the Royal Palace for ever."

"That is my will, Salvis. Meanwhile, the Unseen Lord will carry my power to each person who calls to me."

The rose-coloured light surrounding the third throne stirred. The Unseen Lord was preparing for battle.

Between the Royal Palace and Petroc's farm stood a large, low house which was Carrik's and Esram's home before they went to the far side of the island. At this house the Guardians halted. Tomas dismounted and helped Lindis from her pony.

"Why have we stopped here, Father?" she

29

protested. This house was not as grand as their home on the far side of the island, and Lindis loved the comforts that being Tomas' daughter provided.

"This is where we are to stay, daughter. Lord Bellum will be here to meet us."

A flicker of interest passed across the girl's pretty face. She knew only too well that Lord Bellum was a cruel master, yet Lindis was drawn to him like a moth to a flame.

Carrik's house had been cleaned in readiness and was more comfortable than Lindis had imagined. The floors had carpets and the chairs were padded with cushions of silk.

In a large, airy room stood Lord Bellum, as magnificent as ever, his black hair touching his shoulders, his dark eyes bright and searching. He was dressed in his favourite colours of black and gold, but now, instead of a scarlet serpent, his tabard was emblazoned with a serpent of silver, just like the silver serpents the Guardians wore.

Tomas and Lindis prostrated themselves in a way which made Bellum smile with pleasure, for he desired worship above all things. He did not give them permission to rise, but kept them kneeling at his feet.

"So, Tomas, again we have work to do. You have both served me on the far side of the island, which is now mine. Listen well. The two children from the world beyond the mist are here again. Esram and the boot-maker's daughter, Holly, are here, too. Even now they are on their way to Petroc's farm. We can be sure that the King will send power to his followers, and you must be armed and ready for the battle to win over the people." He touched Lindis with his foot. "Maiden, I desire to give you more of my power."

The girl moved to rise to her feet, but Lord Bellum pushed her back to the floor, telling her to stay where she was. He bent down and placed his hands on her head. Once before he had given her a measure of his own power and she had tried to resist because she had been afraid. She was still afraid, but now she welcomed the waves of cold terror and darkness as they surged relentlessly into her spirit, driving love and compassion away.

When at last she looked up, her dark eyes reflected Bellum's cruelty.

Chapter 4

"We shall fight together"

Petroc's farm had been completely rebuilt. Plump hens ran freely in the yard. A goat was tethered over by the barn. The fields behind the farm provided pasture for many sheep, and the orchard was heavy with blossom, promising much fruit.

Outside the farmhouse door, they paused. Rosie was unexpectedly nervous. She had not been here since the day Tobias had died, when, by his grave, she had first met Salvis.

Luke squeezed her hand. Sometimes, her brother could be a real pain, but there were times, like this, when she was glad he *was* her brother.

"Go in," said Petroc. "The farm is your home, too. You do not have to wait at the door like visitors."

The house brought back so many memories! The smell of cooking, the stone floor, the fire blazing cheerfully; only now, a narrow wooden bed stood in the corner by the hearth and on this bed sat an old lady. Rosie wondered who she was.

Opposite her was a man with grey hair and beard and a weather-beaten face, and Petroc quickly introduced him.

"Uncle Amos, these are my friends, Luke and Rosie, from lands beyond the mist." He explained to Luke, "My uncle has a farm on the far side of the island, but he has been living here to look after us. Soon he will go home. Then the farm will really be mine." This was not a boast, only a simple statement of fact.

"Where's your mother? Where's Martha?" Rosie asked eagerly. The old lady pulled herself from the bed and walked towards them. Her movements were painful and slow but her arms were wide open to greet them.

"Rosie, Luke, can it really be you? You have come back to us after all this long time!"

As she gathered Rosie into her arms, the girl was shocked that this thin, frail old lady with a wrinkled face and grey hair, could be the strong, plump, red-haired Martha who had once taken such good care of them. Then she looked into green eyes, sparkling with joy.

"Martha, I've missed you so much!"

Luke was hugged too, then Esram, and lastly Holly, whom Martha had not met before, but she made her feel just as welcome as the others.

Amos shook each of them by the hand. He was big and he was loud but the love of the King shone from his eyes and Luke instantly liked him.

When all the hugging and hand-shaking was over, they saw that the farm was more comfortable than it used to be. There had never been beds before; they had slept on straw mattresses. Now, the stone floor was warmed by thick rugs, and soft cushions were scattered on the wooden chairs.

One person was missing.

Martha's eyes twinkled. "Morwen has gone out, Luke," she said. "You will most likely find her by the Dark Forest, collecting pine cones for the fire. Those of you who know her should go to find her."

Luke, Rosie and Esram didn't need telling a second time, and Holly had no objection to being left behind, for this meant that she could talk to Petroc. Holly liked Petroc.

They found Morwen where Martha had said she would be, by the forest. She looked up quite suddenly, straight into Luke's eyes, and her face turned very white. She made a strangled sort of noise in her throat, and the pine cones she had been collecting tumbled over the grass.

"I... I cannot believe... It cannot be... Luke! How did you... Why are you..."

For once in his life, Luke was lost for words. His throat was dry and his tongue clung to the roof of his mouth. There had always been something special about Morwen, but now she was even lovelier. She had grown tall and slender and her green eyes were quiet in her oval face. She still wore her red-gold hair in a single braid over one shoulder.

Her beauty did not come from her face, but from within. She had an aura of peace.

Rosie, tired of watching them stare at each other, pushed her brother out of the way.

"Morwen! It's me! I'm here!" she cried.

Morwen regained her composure. "It's so good to see you, Rosie. How did you come back?"

"A long story," Rosie replied. Then, mischievously, because she knew how much Luke had always liked Morwen, and she also knew that Esram liked her, she added, "There's somebody else to see you."

Esram stepped forward, suddenly shy. He and

Morwen looked at each other for what seemed like a long time.

"Morwen," Esram said at last, and in that moment, as he saw Morwen's eyes soften, Luke knew where her heart lay.

"So many children!" Martha exclaimed. "Oh, but it is good to have you all here! I like the house to be full. Supper will soon be ready, so you must wash and change. I have put out clean clothes."

Rosie and Luke looked at each other and they both made a face because they knew what was coming and neither of them wanted to wear island clothes. They had no say in the matter. In Martha's house, young people did as they were told.

Soon they were clean and dry, Luke wearing a green tunic and trousers and grey boots that Petroc had outgrown, and Rosie in a similar outfit of dark turquoise which must once have belonged to Morwen. At least the colours seemed brighter than they used to be! The clothes were actually more comfortable than their own, so it was not so bad.

Martha had her eyes on Rosie's long curls. "All that remains now, child, is for me to plait your hair."

Rosie covered her head with her hands. "Oh Martha, no! The girls on the far side of the island, where we stayed last time, those girls don't plait their hair."

"And a fine mess they are in," Martha snorted. "You are not on the far side of the island, child."

Rosie knew she wouldn't win. "Skinny plaits, then," she said weakly.

"Child?"

"Lots and lots of really thin plaits. Sometimes Stacey does my hair like that at home."

Another snort told her exactly what Martha thought of that idea. She sat Rosie down and began to comb and twist her fair hair, but she plaited so tightly that Rosie squealed.

Morwen laughed. "Shall I do it, Mother? You know how I love to dress hair."

Her mother gave in and turned her attention to Holly, who had been hoping to escape.

"Not me!" she protested, but just like Rosie, she must obey. Here, maidens plaited their hair. By the time supper was ready, Rosie had two braids wound around her head and Holly's plain face was made even more severe by plaited hoops over each ear.

Holly sighed. "At least Salvis loves me," she sighed, aware that unlike Morwen and Rosie, she was not pretty.

"We all love you," Rosie assured her, giving her a hug.

Morwen whispered, "I'll find ribbons for you, Holly, and weave them through your hair. Leave it for now. Supper is nearly ready."

Luke whispered to Rosie. "What d'you bet it's stew?"

He was right. However, Martha's stew was made with many different herbs and exotic vegetables and was delicious. There were no forks. They used chunks of bread as scoops, which was great fun.

Holly made sure she sat next to Petroc, who, with his red hair, tanned skin and green eyes, made up for the discomforts of the farm.

After supper, Luke saw Esram and Petroc take Morwen outside and he guessed that they were passing on the power they had received from the King, as Lord Veritan had told them to do. That had felt weird. When the sword touched his head, Luke knew that something had happened to him, deep inside. He wondered if the others had felt the same.

When they returned, Morwen's eyes were shining with the King's power. She saw Luke watching her and asked him to walk with her across the farmyard.

Outside, the air had grown cool, even though they were in the Time of Plenty, when it was usually very warm.

She slipped her hand through his arm.

"It has been a long time, Luke. So much has happened since the day we last saw you both on the High Moor."

"The farm's looking good. You've done well to rebuild it again," said Luke, trying to change the subject.

"We could not have done it without the King's help. Oh, Luke, we must share stories! Did you have many adventures on the far of the island, with Holly and Esram?"

"Why not ask Esram?"

At last she sensed that all was not well between them. "Luke, we will always be special to each other, will we not? We shared so many hardships when we lived at the Bay of Dolphins. That brought us close in a special way."

"Not like Esram, though?" Luke kicked a stone.

Morwen thought too much of Luke to pretend.

"No, not like Esram," she said, very quietly but firmly. "Esram is more than a friend." She pulled Luke towards her, so that he could not avoid her eyes. "Your future is in your own world, Luke, and there you will meet someone special one day. For me, that someone is Esram and our life is here, on Karensa. It doesn't change how I feel about you. You are my friend and I have thought of you every single day."

They hugged each other, but friendship did not ease the pain in Luke's heart.

Much later, as they all sat around the fire, Morwen threaded ribbons through Holly's hair as she had promised. When she had finished, Holly looked almost pretty in the gentle firelight. Rosie played with the cat. The boys tried to make a football from an old leather sack, which was Luke's idea! It was not as easy as he would have thought.

Martha explained that although she had gone to live on the far side of the island where the climate was kinder to her bones, she could not stay there under the Guardians' control. So, since she also missed her family, she had come home. A friend called Raldi, a carpenter, had made the bed for her, and as long as she kept warm, the pain was bearable.

"I would sooner be in pain than accept the Guardians," she declared with some of her old spirit.

"You may have to accept them," said Petroc, and he told them the news as gently as he was able. "Mother, the Guardians are now here. They are living in Carrik's old house."

The news met with a stunned silence.

"The battle is not over," Amos said sadly. "I had hoped to return to my family before the next Time of Snows."

"You must put them first," Petroc assured him.

Rosie moved closer to Petroc. "We shall fight together," she promised. "Petroc, we'll fight by your side. The Guardians won't win. We shall fight together for the King."

Petroc looked at her as if seeing her for the first time. He had always thought of Rosie as a little child, yet it seemed that she had a strong heart.

"Do you all feel the same?" he asked.

"We do!" they chorused, and Rosie added, "I know this is why we came. Remember what Lord Veritan said to us. Remember the golden sword! I can see it now, in my mind!"

"So can I," Petroc agreed. "I believe we should join hands and think of the sword!"

Amos and Martha watched, not really understanding what they were doing. The young people joined hands, and, holding fast to the picture of the golden sword in their minds, they pledged loyalty to each other and to the King.

Chapter 5

Beneath the cherry tree

As soon as Rosie opened her eyes she remembered where she was and knew what she wanted to do. It was still very early, even for life on the farm. The light filtering through the attic window was grey and cold.

Morwen and Holly were fast asleep so Rosie slipped quietly from beneath the blankets on her straw mattress. She wanted to do this alone. Holly was sleeping on her stomach, and Rosie gently pulled her blankets over her thin shoulders so she would not get too cold. Holly had not thought much of sleeping on straw. In fact, she had complained bitterly.

Rosie picked up her boots and crept down the wooden stairs which were new and shiny. Petroc had said that the upper floor of the farmhouse had only recently been rebuilt.

Downstairs, she was careful not to disturb the sleeping Martha. The front door creaked, but Martha only stirred and turned over, snug and warm in her bed by the kitchen fire.

Rosie pulled on her soft boots and crossed the farmyard. Luke must have had the same idea, for he was already there, and brother and sister knelt at the place where Petroc's father was laid to rest.

At first they knelt in silence, then Rosie said,

"Tobias was kind to us, wasn't he? I can't believe that wooden cross is still there. I made it the day he died."

Luke moved forward and touched it. "The cross will always stand," he murmured.

Rosie knew he was not speaking of two sticks tied together with a red ribbon, but of something much greater.

She closed her eyes and thought of that terrible day when they had buried Tobias. It had snowed as they knelt by his grave. Something soft touched her face. A sudden breeze blew a cloud of late blossom from the cherry tree and the pink and white petals drifted around them and covered the grave.

Neither of them spoke. After a time, they got up and walked down to the farm gate, just as they had done so many times before. To one side was High Hill and beyond it, the sea. In the other direction stood the Dark Forest. Sheep grazed quietly with their lambs in the pasture and corn was shooting up in the fields.

"What d'you think of being back?" Luke asked. It was unusual for him to ask her opinion.

"I don't know... It was all so quick! So much has happened in just one day! We met Petroc, then Esram and Holly, then the Guardians came, then Veritan did that special thing with his sword. I feel I need to stop and get my breath back!"

"Morwen has changed." Luke looked over his sister's shoulder to the Dark Forest.

"So has Esram. He's much taller now. He seems nearly grown up. Holly's changed too. She's not so bossy."

"I wouldn't say that!" her brother laughed.

"We all need to catch up together," Rosie said, frowning. "Petroc... Petroc seems bigger than he used to be."

Luke grinned, because Rosie had a dreamy look in her eyes. "Petroc must be nearly sixteen by now," he pointed out. "You're not yet twelve!"

"I am nearly twelve. And I won't be twelve for ever!"

"We won't be here for ever. We'll go home."

Rosie rested her arms on the farm gate. She could feel the peace of the island all around her.

"I feel as though I've come home," she whispered.

"Don't be – hey! Someone's coming!"

Rosie felt too peaceful to be scared. "Shall I get Amos?" she asked calmly.

She didn't need to fetch Amos because the big, grey haired man was already there, alert to the least sign of danger.

A lone rider approached. He was dressed in the Guardians' uniform of dark grey and blue, the emblem of the silver serpent emblazoned on his tunic and on his shield. He did not consider them worth the trouble of getting down from his horse.

"Do you live on this farm?" he asked. His voice was reasonable and pleasant.

Amos replied that they did.

"I am a messenger. I have come to summon all men to a meeting in the village square, this day at noon. Every man in the area must attend. Our leader, Tomas, wishes to speak with all of you."

Luke and Rosie were uneasy. The soldier had a

mild manner but his message was clear. This was a command, not a request. Already the Guardians were making their presence known.

Petroc, Luke and Esram stood with Amos at the front of the crowd that had gathered in the market square. Many people from the fisher village were here, and many of Petroc's friends from surrounding farms.

The crowd waited impatiently. The day had turned warm and they were all too busy to waste good weather, but they were not to be kept waiting for long. Tomas mounted the platform in the centre of the square and he was taking no chances, for he wore chain mail over his tunic and a helmet covered his corn coloured hair. He was surrounded by soldiers.

He held up his hands for silence.

"People, thank you for coming today! We are the Guardians and I am Tomas, the leader. You will have heard of us. We have brought prosperity to the far side of the island. There, no-one wants for food, nor medicine nor shelter because every need is met from our funds. We believe that the wealthy should help the poor. We have come here to offer our services and our experience to the fisherpeople and the farmers."

He paused. There was a murmur of interest. Esram whispered something to Amos that the others could not hear. Amos raised his hand and spoke up, loud and clear.

"Sir, we follow the King and Lord Salvis here! What of them? Are we to forsake the King to serve the Guardians?"

43

"The King?" Tomas laughed. "Friend, the King will not give you food or look after you when you are sick! You may serve your King, should you wish to, but if you do, you cannot expect to enjoy the benefits we offer!"

Amos shook his head. At that very moment, Tomas noticed Esram and Luke, and as recognition dawned, his eyes narrowed with dislike.

"The Guardians do not tolerate disobedience," he warned. "If by a majority vote you decide to accept us, then all of you must agree to obey Guardian law. You will find this law to be just and fair."

The vote was taken and it was hardly surprising that most hands were raised to accept the Guardians, for life on this side of Karensa was hard, and Tomas promised them freedom from their burdens.

Only a handful of men walked from the meeting in protest, and these were led by Amos and the boys.

Petroc was proud of his uncle.

Luke decided his first impression of Amos had been right and that he could put his trust in this man.

But Esram had once opposed the Guardians and he knew what they were capable of, and Esram's spirit was disturbed. His Uncle Carrik and Reuben had thought they had sent Holly and Esram to safety, but Esram had a feeling that here, they might have to face even worse trouble than before.

Chapter 6

The cost of rebellion

Meanwhile, the girls went to a sandy cove near the farm. The sun was warm on their faces and for a while they were content to search for shells in the rock pools, but Holly was easily bored. She pulled off her boots, and removed her trousers.

"I'm going into the sea," she declared.

As she watched Holly splashing in the waves, Rosie caught sight of two old friends, swimming towards them.

"The dolphins are back!"

The two dolphins swam as near as they could into the shallow water, their grey bodies creating wonderful rainbows of spray with every movement.

Morwen called softly, "Telki, Praze!"

The dolphins stood in the water, chattering with excitement to see old friends.

"They are pleased to see you," said Morwen, who had an understanding of all creatures.

Rosie and Morwen were unable to resist the water any longer. They threw off their boots and trousers and splashed into the sea, paddling as close to Telki and Praze as they could without getting their tunics wet. Young people and dolphins played together, laughing with joy. Telki came so close that Rosie could stroke his smooth, rubbery body.

Then, without warning, the dolphins became distressed and swam off to deep water.

Morwen was puzzled. "Why have they gone?"

"I know why," Holly told her. "Look who's arrived!"

A small figure waved to them from the shore, a girl wearing a tunic of bronze coloured silk, a girl with a pale olive skin, a pretty face and thick, brown hair.

"Oh no," Holly exclaimed. "It's Lindis!"

"Morwen, Lindis is Tomas' daughter," Rosie told her friend. "She's bad news! You don't want to know her!"

Morwen frowned. She could not understand their attitude. Surely they were supposed to behave as Salvis would behave? Morwen knew that Salvis would not send anyone away.

She waved back. "Come in with us!" she called.

Very carefully, and smiling a secret smile, Lindis removed her expensive boots and neatly folded her trousers over them. She always took care of her fine things.

Making scarcely a ripple, she walked out to them and slipped her hand through Holly's arm. Holly shuddered, hating her touch.

Still holding Holly, Lindis addressed Rosie, that smile still on her lips.

"Rosie, you are back," she said softly. "And Holly! You and I were once such friends! We shared many good times together, did we not?"

Holly stared at her. "Did we, Lindis? Well, maybe times have changed. We have not spoken for over a year!"

"What are you both doing here?" Lindis asked innocently.

"Visiting." Holly knew too much about Lindis to trust her with any information.

"Do you remember the time we found that perfume, Holly? Oh, we were such children then!" Lindis giggled.

"I do remember it. That was the day you fell into the pig pen. The pig smell suited you better than the perfume!"

Lindis detached her hand from Holly's arm. "I did not fall into the pig pen. You pushed me."

Holly grinned. "What, like this?" She gave Lindis a hard shove so that the other girl sprawled backwards into the sea.

Lindis got up, coughing and spluttering. Seaweed was hanging from one ear. She pushed Holly, who fell over too, then Rosie, then Morwen, who was trying to stop them.

"You will regret this!" Lindis spluttered. "You do not desire my friendship. So be it. Soon you will need my help. New laws will be passed and you will not be able to serve your King!"

As she uttered this threat, Morwen caught her eye and she knew why Holly and Rosie disliked her. She felt sick, because when she looked into Lindis' eyes, there was no doubt in Morwen's mind that this girl served Lord Bellum.

On their way back through the Dark Forest, Amos strode in front. The boys walked in a group together.

"What do you think will happen to us?" Luke asked.

Esram shrugged. "You know what the Guardians are like. They won't do anything to hurt us. They will just make it impossible for us to live."

"They said their law was just," said Petroc.

"So it is," Luke agreed, remembering when he and Rosie had lived on the far side of the island. "The law is OK, it's how they use it that's wrong. They make the law do what they want it to do. Their law didn't allow them to put people to death, yet it did allow them to set Carrik and Esram adrift in a boat so they were sure to drown."

Esram had not told Petroc about this. "This must be why the King sent Veritan to us," Petroc mused.

"Maybe," Luke agreed.

Esram added, "We shall need that strength. I feel we have been brought together to support each other, and to protect the farm. I believe the King has a special purpose for your farm, Petroc."

"Yes, that is how I feel," Petroc agreed, with a greater respect for Esram.

"And Luke," the older boy went on. "Luke, you are very much a part of this. The King is saying that it was for such a time as this that he brought you here."

Luke stared at Esram and realised that, like Morwen, there was so much love for Salvis in Esram that he was able to hear the King's voice clearly. He lived only to serve him.

"We are still brothers, Luke?" Petroc asked.

"We are all brothers now," said Luke. "Give me your hands."

The three boys clasped their hands and promised friendship.

Morwen, Rosie and Holly stood in a very wet line.

"You are dripping water all over the floor," Martha complained. "I dare not ask what you have been doing. I do not want to set eyes on you again until you are dry and in clean clothes."

"It wasn't our fault, and at least our trousers didn't get wet," said Holly, taking no notice of Rosie who warned her to be quiet.

Martha rose to her feet. Her face was stern. She might be old and frail, but when she looked at them in such a way, the girls did as they were told.

By the time supper was ready, Morwen had found Rosie a yellow tunic and Holly a pink one, and their hair was washed in the tub of water that was always kept hot over the fire in the outhouse. Rosie pulled her own hair into a single high plait and Morwen braided Holly's hair and wound the braids around her head in a circlet, weaving into it a long, pink ribbon. The style did suit her. It made her hazel eyes look bigger.

Supper that evening was a noisy meal. Everyone shared what had happened to them and their natural reaction to the coming trouble was to make as much noise as they could, to block it from their minds.

Martha and Amos sat together and watched the young people enjoying themselves. Morwen was making music on a reed instrument. Rosie was trying, not very successfully, to teach Petroc the dance steps of her favourite boy band, but the music was wrong and Petroc had no sense of rhythm.

"Do you want to try?" Luke asked Holly.

"Not me!" she shook her head. "I'll play the music, then Morwen and Esram can dance."

She and Morwen changed places. Holly played well, and Esram took Morwen's hand.

"We danced before, Morwen, remember?" he whispered.

Morwen was suddenly shy. "I said I did not know the steps."

"And I said I would teach you."

Holly played slowly as the boy and girl moved across the floor of the farmhouse. Their eyes never left each other as they danced, Morwen following Esram's every move. Time stood still for them as they were lost in their secret memories.

Rosie nudged her brother. "Ask her to dance! Cut in!" she whispered urgently.

"No. Morwen should dance with Esram now."

Rosie felt sorry for him and gave his arm a squeeze. He wished she hadn't. It made him feel worse.

The music ended and Holly sat by Luke's side.

"So, Luke, how are things in your world? Do you have a maiden of your own yet?" Holly never minced her words.

"There is one... Rachel."

Holly looked at Morwen then back to Luke. "Morwen is too tall and thin for you," she observed. "You need a maiden who is round and small."

Luke gave a sort of half smile. "Rachel is small and roundish."

Holly replied carefully, "Rachel is a nice name."

"So is Holly. You are small, but not round," he answered.

There was an awkward silence and now it was her turn to blush. "My mother named me Holly because I was born during the Time of Snows."

"Do you still miss your mother?"

"I always will, I suppose. What about you?"

"Me too. Stacey, my stepmother, she's nice, but it's not the same."

"No," she agreed. "It's not the same."

At that moment there was a loud knocking at the front door. Amos gestured to them to stay where they were and opened the door. Three Guardians stood there. One of them had a scroll in his hand.

"Who is the owner of this farm?" he wanted to know.

Petroc stepped forward. "The farm is mine. What is your business here?"

If the man was surprised that the farm belonged to a fifteen-year-old boy, he didn't show it.

"We have been sent to visit the homes of all those who walked from the meeting this morning, to advise them that the following laws have been passed."

"Go on," said Petroc, swallowing the sick feeling in his throat.

The soldier read from the scroll. "First, *none shall buy or sell unless they wear the emblem of the silver serpent...* Second, *all must pay taxes towards the upkeep of the Guardians. Those refusing to wear the silver serpent will pay double the amount...* Third, *no meeting to be held unless called by the Guardians...* Now, will you pledge your allegiance to the Guardians and wear the silver serpent?"

Another Guardian held out a silver wristband in the shape of a serpent. The tail threaded through a lock just below the head so that the head would extend across the back of the hand. "See, once on your wrist it is impossible to remove this without a key, and only Guardians have keys. It cannot be stolen or borrowed. Without this bracelet you cannot buy or sell goods. Wear this and you shall trade freely and your tax burden will be light."

Petroc spoke for them all. "We will have no serpent here. We are followers of the King in this house."

"So be it, but you will discover the cost of rebellion."

They left abruptly. Petroc closed the door and leant back against it, suddenly fearful for the future.

"Uncle Amos, what shall we do? We cannot take our produce to market and we cannot buy food. We shall have no income. How can we pay this tax?"

Morwen added, "We are not allowed to call meetings. How can our friends come here to praise the King?"

They stared at each other in despair.

"Well," said Esram, "we must praise him now."

So they did; their songs were a plea for help, and in the Royal Palace, the King heard them and sent the Unseen Lord to them, and their strength was renewed.

Chapter 7

Carrik's house

Weeks passed and at first life continued in much the same way as it had always done. At the end of the first month, two Guardians arrived to collect their taxes, which were taken from the small amount of money Amos held in reserve. They lived on food from their store. Life was deceptively normal.

One morning, Petroc asked Luke to go with him to the top field. He wanted to make sure the fences were safe, because sometimes deer from the Dark Forest damaged the fences and sheep strayed.

It was warm. Luke was content. One day he and Rosie would return to Cornwall, but he was in no hurry to go back. Life there held its own problems, like school exams and career choices.

As they walked, the boys talked over old times. Then, "You know my sister and Esram are becoming close?" Petroc asked. He guessed how Luke felt about Morwen and didn't want him to be hurt.

"Yes, I've seen it, too. They are... they suit each other, I feel." There were times when Luke drifted into island speech without realising he had done so.

"You and she were once friends."

"We're still friends," said Luke and made it clear that he didn't want to talk about Morwen.

When they reached the field, Petroc went one

way and Luke the other, so that they would eventually meet in the middle. Petroc trusted him to complete the task, so Luke was extra careful as he scrutinised the woven branches.

He was intent on his work when he heard a cry from the track below. He stood up, shading his eyes against the sun, and he saw Lindis at the bottom of the hill. She was leading her pony and she was limping badly.

"Luke! Oh please, come and help me!"

Her voice was pitiful, but Luke was wary as he walked down the hill.

"What is it, Lindis?"

"Oh Luke, I'm so glad it's you." She opened her dark eyes very wide. "The others do not like me. I've twisted my ankle and cannot walk. Could you help me mount up and then lead my pony a little way, just to make sure I'm safe to ride?"

There seemed no harm in that, so Luke agreed and didn't bother to tell Petroc where he was going. After all, he didn't plan to go far.

Petroc worked his way around the fence, thinking how good it was to have Luke and Rosie back. He had missed Luke, who had been his first real friend. And Rosie had grown up such a lot in the time they had been away! There was something special about Rosie. She understood his passion for his farm.

He was unprepared for the shock of seeing two Guardians watching him, and couldn't hold back a cry of surprise. He looked round for Luke, who had disappeared.

"What do you want? This is my land!"

"You are to come with us," they told him. "We

have been sent by Tomas to fetch you. He desires to speak with you."

"I do not desire to speak with him!" Petroc retorted. Without further ado, they both drew their swords and held one to his back, the other to his throat. He was forced to ride pillion as they took a narrow track through the Dark Forest towards the house that belonged to Carrik in the days before he served the King.

Petroc tried to keep calm, but this reminded him of that day long ago when he had been taken down this very same track. Months of captivity had followed, first in Carrik's house and later in Lord Bellum's stronghold. He told himself that this would not happen again. Under his breath, he began to speak in the special words he had received from the King when he made Salvis his lord. This strange language reminded him that whatever happened, Salvis was with him.

The house was not far. There, Petroc was taken to a large room where two men were waiting for him. One was Tomas, who sat at a polished table. The other man stood with his back to him, looking out of the window.

"So this is Petroc," Tomas said, in that pleasant voice which deceived many. "I have heard a lot about you, Petroc."

"Who from?" Petroc found it difficult to speak. The house reminded him of the time when he had been a prisoner here. He had hoped never to see it again.

"From me, Petroc." The other man turned around and Petroc's knees very nearly gave way as he looked into the eyes of Bellum, the Lord of all Darkness.

When the room had stopped spinning, Petroc stood as tall as he could and faced his old enemy. Bellum had been a Lord of the Palace until he disobeyed the King and brought separation between the King and his people that only the death of the King's son, Salvis, could heal.

"You look well, Petroc," said Bellum. Today, his voice was friendly, but Petroc knew it could change at any moment. Bellum could roar like a lion in anger, or hiss like the serpent he had taken as his emblem.

"You must kneel before Lord Bellum!" Tomas ordered.

Bellum held up his hand. "Not so. I shall not force him to kneel. One day he will worship me of his own free will."

"I will not!"

"Well, we shall see." Bellum sounded amused.

Something about Bellum always made Petroc determined to resist him, even when he was afraid.

"You know I shall never serve you. My life is promised to the King. I shall never change."

"Never is a long time, Petroc. For the moment, your farm prospers, but in time you may find it hard without the serpent for your protection. I have a proposal. Come back now to my castle and your family may trade again. They need not wear the silver serpent on their hands."

It was a clear choice; the silver serpent or the golden sword. Petroc didn't have to think about which one to choose.

"My family would not accept that proposal!"

"Come back with me now, Petroc," Bellum persuaded. "I will give you everything you need. You will rule by my side."

"The King rules Karensa!"

"Not everywhere and not for ever. I could fulfil your heart's desire, Petroc, if you embrace the serpent."

Petroc felt sick. Once again, the room began to spin.

Suddenly, for no reason at all, Petroc laughed. He had no idea what was so amusing. Bellum's black eyes glinted as he struggled to hold back his anger.

"Go then!" he said abruptly. "When you have stopped laughing, I shall be waiting. Only do not take too long to make up your mind!"

"I have made up my mind!" said Petroc, still laughing as he walked freely from the room.

Tomas turned to Bellum. "Lord, what is so special about this boy? Why do you need him?"

"I do not need him, Tomas. Once Petroc defied me and the might of my stronghold could not break the spirit of a thirteen-year-old boy. I will have him back, no matter what the cost. I will not be defied!"

Luke accompanied Lindis to the place where the track narrowed into the Dark Forest.

"You seem OK," he observed.

"I shall do well enough now. It's been good to see you again, Luke."

Luke nodded. He had never thought Lindis was as bad as Holly and Rosie said. She smiled her thanks and rode away, leaving him wondering about her.

He turned back to see how Petroc was doing, but there was no sign of his friend. He must have finished the fence on his own and gone home. Luke decided to follow.

When he arrived at the farm, Holly and Morwen, who had been in the yard all morning, said they hadn't seen Petroc.

Morwen looked worried. "I have a bad feeling about this. If he is not back soon, we should go to look for him."

Chapter 8

Enemy or friend?

Lord Bellum was waiting for Lindis in the room where Petroc had been taken. She fell on her knees and covered her face, for she could see that Bellum was not in a good mood. Her natural response was to hide. Perversely, he told her to rise, so she stood, trembling, before him.

"You would speak with me, master?"

Bellum's ringed fingers tapped the arms of his chair.

"Tell me what you know of this boy, Petroc," he demanded.

Lindis did her best to hide her feelings, but Bellum was too quick for her.

"Ah, Lindis, I see you like the boy?"

"He is a simple farm boy," she replied evasively.

Bellum was not deceived. "You like the boy," he stated.

"I do, master."

"What would you do to make him your own? What lengths would you go to?"

"Master?"

"Would you persuade him to come back to my castle with you? He would be my highest servant."

The idea excited her. "How could that be? Petroc is determined to stay a King's man."

"Maiden," the Lord of Darkness laughed softly, "maiden, do not underestimate my power. You have that power in abundance! You will deceive him. He will never be sure if you are his enemy or his friend! Then, when he is in my castle, you may do with him as you will. When you are both old enough, make him your husband! Or make him your slave!"

"How can he be my slave? You will have promised him the highest position in your household."

Again the laugh. "Promises or lies, what difference does it make? I will have Petroc, of that you may be sure, and the day he enters my castle of his own free will, that day I will give you all you desire. Do you agree to help me, Lindis?"

Lindis drew a picture of Petroc in her mind. Her excitement increased.

"I will help you, master. What shall I do?"

Bellum gave a smile of satisfaction. If she had refused, he would have forced her to obey him, but this was the better way. This way she would desire more and more of his power and he would give that when it suited his plans.

"First, little daughter, you must win his trust... "

Petroc's laughter faded as he walked through the Dark Forest. He had the strangest feeling he was being watched. Although he couldn't see anyone, he was uneasy. A sudden movement in the thicket startled him. It was only a deer. He quickened his pace, anxious to reach open fields where he would be safe from ambush.

He was disturbed that he had been captured so easily. They would all need to be more alert, and never go out on their own. Today, Bellum had released him, but he could have made him his prisoner. The thought of going back into Bellum's dark castle sent a shiver down his spine.

Petroc didn't see the three youths until it was too late. They surrounded him. They were all bigger and older than he, and he didn't recognise any of them. Maybe they had come with the Guardians?

The biggest youth grabbed Petroc's wrist. "Why do you not wear the silver serpent?"

Petroc would not let them see he was afraid.

"I don't wear the serpent because I am the King's man and always will be!"

"Then we must show you what happens to the King's men. They are not wanted any more!"

They closed in on him. Their faces were menacing. Petroc knew what was coming and braced himself, for he could not fight back. Two of them held him while the biggest youth delivered kicks and blows.

As he sank to the ground, he was dimly aware of Lindis riding towards him, screaming at the youths. Then a curtain came down and everything went dark.

He didn't see Lindis press a gold coin into each of the youths' hands and smile at them before they ran away.

The dark curtain lifted slowly as he struggled to open his eyes. He could taste blood. His body hurt in every place it could possibly hurt. Blood trickled down his face and into his mouth. As the world swung back into focus, he saw a girl's face very close to his own.

Lindis was crying as she dabbed his wounds.

"Petroc, oh, say you are alive! Oh, how could they do this to you? They have really hurt you! I will have them caught and punished! My father shall punish them!"

With the help of Lindis and a nearby tree, Petroc pulled himself into a sitting position, but the Dark Forest was swaying from side to side. When he tried to speak, the words left his mouth as a low moan of pain.

Lindis sat back on her heels. Her rich silk tunic was splattered with blood, but for once, she didn't seem to care about her clothes.

"We have to get you home," she said. "Could you ride?"

Another moan.

"Rest a moment then. I shall fetch a drink."

He leant back against a tree and closed his eyes. She returned with a container, which she held to his lips. The water was cold and sweet. He drank deeply and his head cleared.

"Shall we try?" Her voice was ever so gentle.

Somehow, Petroc scrambled onto the pony, slumped over its neck and clinging desperately to its mane.

Lindis led the pony, stopping every little while to give Petroc a rest and a drink of water, and in this way they made a slow journey back to the farm. Esram and Luke ran to the gate to meet them.

Petroc tried to speak. "Lindis, you must... come in..."

Lindis shook her head, smiling sadly, and allowing a small tear to slide down her cheek. "I would not be made welcome. Your friends will help you now."

"I... Thank you... " was all Petroc could say as, with a brief acknowledgement of her help, Esram and Luke took over and carried Petroc across the yard.

As she watched them take Petroc home, Lindis smiled again that secret smile. Everything had gone according to plan. Pleased with her day's work, she rode away.

Rosie never forgot how she felt when Esram and Luke laid Petroc on Martha's bed. She knelt by his side, holding his hand and refusing to move while Martha and Morwen attended to his wounds. Tears were streaming down Rosie's cheeks, for she knew now how much she cared about him. She never wanted to leave him. She never wanted to go home.

That night they broke Guardian law and invited a few of their friends, the ones they could trust, to a meeting to cry to the King to help them.

Petroc was seated in a chair by the fire. He was bandaged and clean, and although his body hurt all over, he felt better after a bowl of Martha's broth. His head ached, but that was not going to stop him from joining in the meeting.

People gathered in silence, knowing the danger they were in if the Guardians discovered them, afraid of what the future held, yet determined to praise their King.

Amos opened the meeting. "My dear friends," he said, his voice heavy with emotion, "this is only the beginning. We shall need to support each other in days to come. Even more important, we must all ask the King to help us. This is a battle we cannot fight on our own. We cannot survive without each other and we cannot survive without the King! And... and more than that... will you all ask the King to help me, for I am so angry that this has happened! Salvis taught us not to be angry in this way, but... but..." He fell on his knees and some of the men gathered round him, asking the King to help him.

Morwen took her lyre and they sang in praise of the King. They had never exalted the King, or cried to him for help, in such a way as they did that night. Afterwards, some said the colour of the light changed as the Unseen Lord washed over each one of them in a torrent of love and power until each person was refreshed and renewed.

Rosie's eyes never left Petroc, even though she was singing with the others.

Petroc was thinking about Lindis. Was she an enemy or a friend? His spirit told him she was their enemy. His eyes told him she was his friend.

Holly stayed close to Luke. She would never admit it, but she was just a little afraid, for she had never called to the King in such a way.

Luke and Esram were lost in wonder as they became increasingly aware of the King's presence.

Morwen's eyes were closed and she dared not open them, for if she did, she thought she might see Salvis himself in all his glory. He was so close to them all.

Chapter 9

The Time of Gathering

It was midnight by the time the last person left the meeting. Petroc looked very pale and tired and Rosie knelt by his chair.

"You look like a wounded soldier, Petroc," she said sadly. "You should be resting."

"I am rested," he answered weakly. "I've never felt Salvis so close to me as I did tonight. But I am tired." He lifted his hand to his head. Blood was seeping through the bandage. "Everything I touch seems to hurt!"

"You must sleep in my bed tonight," his mother declared. "I shall sleep upstairs, with the girls."

"No, Mother," Morwen told her firmly. "The last thing we need is you being ill again. Sleep in your own bed, Mother. We can make Petroc a bed on the floor, in front of the fire."

Her mother looked as though she was going to argue, but Holly whispered to her, "You will be at Petroc's side and can tend his needs."

"Very well," Martha agreed. "Luke, Esram, shall you fetch Petroc's bedding down?"

Before the boys could move, there was a loud knocking on the door. Everyone froze, terrified that the Guardians had heard of their meeting and had come to arrest them.

"Amos, it is me, Raldi! See what I have found!"

With a sigh of relief, Amos opened the door to their oldest friend.

"I found this on the fence by the gate." Raldi handed Amos a wide necked bottle.

Amos pulled the cork and sniffed the bottle. "I have not seen this for a long time!" he exclaimed.

Luke was curious. "What is it?" he asked.

Amos handed him the bottle. The contents looked like custard but smelled of lemons and strawberries and apricots.

"This is that stuff Salvis gave me when I was hurt!" he cried.

As the others crowded round, Martha felt it was time she took control. Shoo-ing them out of the way, she asked Rosie to fetch a beaker, then, while Rosie held the beaker, Martha poured out the thick, yellow liquid.

"It is a special medicine which is found only on Karensa," Martha explained. "When Bellum disobeyed the King, the medicine disappeared. Now only Salvis can supply it."

If Salvis alone could supply the medicine, and it had been found by the farm gate, that must mean...

"Now Rosie," Martha went on, her voice shaking a little. "Take the beaker and give it to Petroc."

With everyone watching her, Rosie was suddenly shy. She lifted the beaker to Petroc's mouth. His lips were swollen and bruised, but he managed to drain the cup and at once some colour returned to his face. Seeing how anxious Rosie looked, he held her hand.

"Rosie, I feel Salvis wants you to know he is with you, and will stay with you always, no matter what the future holds. He has promised to never leave us or forsake us."

That Petroc should think of her needs rather than his own pain made Rosie burst into tears.

After that night, Petroc's wounds healed swiftly. Some said it was because he was strong and healthy. Some said the King had healed him. His friends didn't really mind which was right, just as long as he recovered.

All through the long, hot days of the Time of Plenty, Luke and Rosie worked on the farm. Their faces turned brown and their eyes were bright and healthy.

Neither Luke nor Rosie was in a hurry to leave Karensa. In the past, when they had come to the island, they had worried about when they could go home, but this time they felt differently.

Rosie didn't even want to go home, not only because she didn't want to leave Petroc, but because her spirit was now one with the island. She loved being here, so close to Salvis. They couldn't see him, but he was always there, his presence brooding over them and helping them. From the top of High Hill she could see the turrets of the Royal Palace, where Salvis lived. At those times, he was especially near.

Luke was in no great hurry to go home for different reasons. He knew that the time was coming when he must make decisions about his future. During the next school year he would take his exams and then he must decide which way to go. His teachers advised him one thing, but his heart told him something quite different.

Sometimes he and Rosie would talk about Dad and Stacey and Pepper and their friends at Poldawn, and then they would both feel homesick, but only for a little while. They now thought of Karensa as their true home.

Life became harder for those people who remained loyal to the King. The new laws made it almost impossible for them to live. Farmers were better off than most, for they had their own produce for food. Petroc, Esram and Luke added to this by going fishing each evening. Even so, there were times when they were hungry, and times also when they were asked to give from their own food store to those without food. To give to others and go hungry themselves was especially hard.

They would be able to pay their taxes until the Time of Snows, but after that, their savings would be spent. Since they could not trade, they would lose the farm.

In spite of all this, or perhaps because of it, Salvis was as close to them as when he had lived at the Bay of Dolphins.

The Time of Plenty mellowed into the Time of Gathering. Days were warm, and although harvesting was hard work, it was also fun. The children ended each day with hay fights, while Amos and Martha watched indulgently, pleased to see them being children for a little while.

Morwen and Esram rarely joined in the fun, preferring to walk on their own along the cliff top or to High Hill.

It was on High Hill that Morwen persuaded

Esram to tell her about how Luke and the other children had rescued Esram and Carrik on the far side of the island. She knew the Guardians tried to set them adrift, hoping they would drown.

"I thought I would die that day," he told her. "All I could think of was coming back to the farm. This is the only place I've ever been really happy."

Morwen was silent. What a strange life Esram had led! He couldn't remember his parents. He had been brought up by his Uncle Carrik, who had then been a harsh, greedy man serving Lord Bellum. Carrik had put Morwen's own father to death. But then, first Esram and then Carrik had given their lives to the King and could not wait to spread the good news that Salvis was alive, and he was willing to forgive those who turned back to the King.

Esram loved to tell people this and show them how to ask Salvis to fill their hearts with his special peace, which was like nothing anyone could ever imagine.

"My uncle killed your father," he said slowly, as if he was reading her thoughts.

"The King has forgiven him," she replied, freely and without hesitation. "So must we."

Esram shook his head. "I know you have forgiven us, Morwen, but sometimes I can hardly believe it."

She moved closer to him. "We have forgiven you," she repeated. "Esram ... you are our friend. You will always be our friend."

"I want to be more than your friend, Morwen," Esram whispered, and lifting her hands, he kissed them softly.

Morwen blushed and pulled her hands away.

At last the harvest was gathered and safely stored in the barn. Work was over for the time being. It was midday and they were hot and sticky.

"Let's go to the beach to cool down," Luke suggested, and everyone agreed, so they made their way to the sandy cove where the girls had played with the dolphins.

Morwen and Esram sat on the rocks, their arms around each other, lost in a world of their own.

The others rolled up their trousers and paddled, jumping over the waves, seeing how far out they could go without getting wet. Luke was the first to get bored. He found some long, slimy seaweed and threw it at Holly, who squealed when it wrapped itself around her head.

"I shall smell of fish!" she protested and threw it back to him, but she missed and he picked it up again and threw it at Rosie.

"Ugh! It's all slippery!" She pulled it from her hair. "I'll get you for this, Luke!"

He laughed loudly as the others chased him up the beach. Petroc brought him down. Rosie sat on his feet and Petroc held his arms while Holly stuffed seaweed down the neck of his tunic. He was too helpless with laughter to resist.

Suddenly, Holly stopped. She pulled the tunic aside to reveal the long, white scar on Luke's shoulder.

"Where did you get that?"

Petroc released Luke's arms. "He got it trying to rescue me from Bellum," he told her.

Rosie got off her brother's feet and he sat up. He

was not laughing any more. "Petroc gave himself up to save me, Holly," he said.

For a long time they sat quietly. Remembering the past made them think of a future that was uncertain.

Rosie decided that this was getting too serious. She attacked Petroc with the seaweed, but he was big enough to pick her up, throw her over his shoulder and twirl her around until she screamed.

They didn't see a small figure watching them from the cliffs. Lindis wanted to join in. A small part of her wished she had never accepted Lord Bellum as her master. She thought all love had been driven from her heart, but it had not, because she longed for friendship.

It was too late now to change her mind. She saw Rosie and Petroc laughing together and was jealous, and determined that Rosie must be removed before she spoilt her plans.

Chapter 10

An empty net

As soon as they had eaten their supper, the boys set off with their rods and nets. They fished from a headland on the other side of the village. It was quite a long way from the farm, but this headland went so far out to sea that fish were plentiful. Many people fished there. It was worth the long walk because no-one ever went home empty-handed.

Tonight's catch would be tomorrow's supper. This, with their own fruit, vegetables and grain, milk and cheese from the goat, and eggs from the hens, would provide for them if they were careful.

Martha had wisely rationed their food to one main meal each evening. Breakfast was either a small bowl of porridge or fresh bread and eggs. Food stocks would need to last as long as possible. Their present lambs were too small for slaughter and the hens were needed for eggs. Fish was a valuable addition to their diet.

Petroc and Luke walked a little way ahead. They never meant Esram to feel left out, and if he did feel like that, he was too good-natured to let it spoil their friendship. Esram was content to walk alone. He could always think about Morwen.

Esram and Morwen no longer tried to hide their feelings for each other and they could be seen holding hands at every given opportunity. Holly would make faces behind their backs, sticking her fingers down her throat and pretending to be sick. Secretly, Luke was hurt to see Esram with Morwen because he still liked Morwen very much.

Petroc had mixed feelings about Esram. He had forgiven him, but he did not find it easy to forget how cruel Esram had once been, or that his Uncle Carrik had killed Petroc's own father. Salvis had taught them to forgive, but Petroc found it hard to forget.

The boys passed the fisher village and turned to follow the path over the cliffs leading to the headland, but tonight something was wrong. The way had been blocked by a high wall of heavy stones.

"The path has always been open. Who can have done this?" Petroc muttered, running his fingers through his red hair so that it stuck out in a tangle.

"Is there no other way to the headland?" Luke asked.

"None that I know of. This is the only path we can take."

Esram caught up with them. "This has to be the work of the Guardians," he declared. "This is the sort of thing they do."

Just as he spoke, a man's voice challenged them and two Guardians approached them, both wearing full uniform with chain mail and drawn swords. They were the same men who had taken Petroc to Tomas' house to meet Bellum. Petroc's hand moved to the small fishing knife hidden beneath his cloak. They would not take him prisoner a second time without a fight.

"This path is closed! You cannot go any further!" they were told.

"By whose authority is it closed, sir?" asked Esram, who knew the way to speak to the Guardians.

"By order of Tomas, our leader."

"Why? Why is it closed? We have only come here to fish. Where is the harm in that?" Petroc protested.

Luke, thinking of life back home, added, "If this is a public footpath, you have no legal right to close it. You have to let us through."

The Guardians laughed derisively. They did not even bother to answer, and Luke felt rather silly.

"Go home," they were advised. "If you do not turn away now, we shall have no choice but to arrest you. We have built a new prison in the village for those who break our law."

Petroc would have liked to argue, but Luke and Esram pulled him away. Once inside the Guardians' prison, they could be kept there until Tomas decided to release them. That could be weeks, months, or years. Or never.

They turned away with the sound of the Guardians' mocking laughter in their ears.

One of the Guardians shouted after them. "Boys should not try to do men's work!"

This hurt them more than their hunger.

With a dramatic gesture, Petroc threw his empty net on the kitchen table, declaring that there would be no more fish.

Amos sensed they were afraid as well as troubled.

"What has happened?" he asked anxiously. It was unusual for Petroc to reveal his fears.

All three began to talk at once and Amos held up his hand for silence. "One at a time, one at a time. Petroc, calm down! Luke, you tell me what is wrong."

Luke explained what had happened. "We shall have no more fish for supper," he sighed.

There was silence as everyone received the news that another blow had been struck against them.

Petroc's anger flared. "We do not have to accept this! We should not be treated in this way!" he cried fiercely. "We do not want these Guardians here. Veritan used the golden sword to empower us. It is time we learnt to fight against them!"

"No, that cannot be what Lord Veritan meant! It is not the way," Morwen protested urgently. Her brother worried her when he was in this reckless mood. She feared for his safety. "Petroc, you know Salvis would want us to have victory by trusting in him. He wants us to win people over to his side by living in peace, no matter what others do to us. The power is to help us stay true!"

Luke and Rosie recalled that they had received much the same teaching in church at home, and they were inclined to agree with Morwen.

"You were not even there, Morwen!" Petroc shouted, and then he went out, slamming the door behind him and ignoring his own rule that no-one should venture out alone. As he did so often when he was hurt or confused, he went to High Hill.

From there, just as he had done so many times before, he watched the sun fading behind the mist. For a while the island was bathed in a pink light; soft shadows tinged with gold in the Dark Forest.

Karensa was his home and below was his farm

and he felt a fierce love for both. He also felt the first chill of the approaching Time of Snows. In the cold, dark days that lay ahead, they were going to be tested to the limit.

He dropped to his knees, looked towards the Royal Palace and with his hands held high he made a solemn promise.

"Lord King, you have said you always hear us when we call to you! Hear me now! I swear before you that none shall ever take my farm from me. I swear before you that none shall ever force me to wear that serpent on my hand. I shall stay true always to the golden sword! Lord King, help me! Show me the way to defeat these men! Show me how to fight the Guardians, even if I must fight alone." He lowered his voice to a faint whisper. "Salvis, show me the way. Help me be rid of the Guardians, whatever it takes."

The sun disappeared, and darkness covered the land.

Chapter 11

Rosie

The very next morning, when Morwen went to milk the goat, its tethering rope was empty. The goat had gone. The rope had been cut with a knife.

Morwen went to the kitchen to tell the others, reluctant to be the bearer of such terrible news.

"It is no use searching for her," she concluded. "Someone has stolen her, that's for sure. Now we have no milk, no cheese and no fish!"

Amos put his hand on her shoulder. "Maiden, no-one could have stolen our goat. The dog sleeps in the barn. He would have barked and seen off any intruder."

Luke's face turned deep crimson. He hung his head. "The dog slept indoors last night," he admitted. "It was cold, so I let him sleep with me." He missed his collie, Pepper. The farm dog had comforted him.

Holly glared at him. She screwed up her eyes and put her hands on her hips.

"Luke! How could you have been so stupid?" she cried.

"I don't know," he muttered. What else could he say?

Morwen came to his rescue. "Maybe dogs are allowed to sleep indoors where Luke comes from? That doesn't solve our problem, though. We are going to be desperately short of food. We cannot

77

survive for ever on vegetables, bread and a few eggs. We cannot buy food unless we wear the Guardians' mark, even if we had the money. What shall we do, Uncle?"

Amos shook his head. "I do not know... Maiden, it is beyond my understanding. What *can* we do?"

"Well," said Luke, "I have an idea... "

The market square had changed. The village was more prosperous now. Folk stood chatting to each other as though they had all the time in the world. Life was easier under Guardian law. The market stalls were colourful and sold a variety of goods; pots and pans, rich material of silk or wool, tempting cakes and pies; one stall even sold toys; hoops and dolls, spinning tops and polished marbles.

Looming above this new-found prosperity, the new prison reminded everyone of the Guardians' authority. It was rumoured there were already prisoners held there.

"I don't think we did the right thing," Rosie said to Luke. "Somehow I don't think we'll be able to buy and sell here."

"After what I did with the dog, we have to try. If the dog had been in the barn, no-one could have stolen the goat. It's down to me to do something to put it right. We are not from Karensa. We might get served without wearing that serpent thing."

Rosie sighed. He's wrong, she thought.

Six days had passed since the goat had been stolen and now Martha was even more careful with their rations, fearing to use up what little food they had. Most of the time, the young people were hungry.

It had been Luke's idea that he and Rosie should come to the market to buy the meat they needed.

"What have we got to lose?" he argued when Martha and Amos both expressed their misgivings. "They can't hurt us for trying, can they? We won't be breaking their precious law! What can they do to us for looking around the market? If they do throw us in prison, well then, at least we'll get a good meal!" he added.

Martha didn't approve of such talk. "You should not make fun of the Guardians," she rebuked him. "They are not to be taken lightly. You do not know their ways."

"We do, Martha, dear." Rosie threw her arms around this woman she had grown to love. "We found out what the Guardians were really like on the far side of the island. We will go anyway, Martha. It will be all right, really it will!"

Martha disentangled herself. "And what do you propose to use for money? We cannot spend our savings. That money will be needed for our next tax payment."

As they looked at each other for inspiration, Martha removed the slim gold chain she always wore.

"If you are really determined to go, then you must take this. It is not worth a great deal of money, but it should be enough to buy a store of meat."

"Mother!" Petroc protested. "My father gave you that necklace. It is the only jewellery you possess. I know how much it means to you. You cannot sell it!"

But Morwen, understanding Martha as only a

daughter could, accepted the gold chain. "Are you quite sure, Mother? It is your last memory of Father."

"Oh no, daughter. My memories of Tobias are in my heart."

Esram, who until now had been silent, held Martha's hand. She had become so thin that her hand was lost in his own.

"You have given everything you have, Martha," he said. "The King will be sure to bless you for this."

"I hope so, Esram," Martha sighed. "I hope he blesses us with food. And safety for Luke and Rosie, of course."

"The King will do things his way," said Esram mysteriously.

So here they were, very unsure and more than a little afraid. If only they could have seen one friendly face in the people who pushed and jostled around each market stall!

"There's a butcher over there," said Luke, holding tightly to his sister's hand to give her courage.

Rosie approached the butcher, who was a thin, wiry man and did not look like a butcher at all. She pointed to a tray of sausages, which were the only things she knew how to ask for among a bewildering display of meat. Rosie didn't know one cut of meat from another.

"How much are your sausages, please? Will you take this in payment?" She held out the gold chain. "It must be worth far more than your sausages.

Would you take this and give us some money back in return, please?"

The man looked her up and down. "I do not recognise either of you, and others are waiting to be served. I cannot waste time with necklaces," he told her sourly.

"We're strangers," Luke explained. "We don't belong here. Our home is far away."

The butcher's hand darted forward and lifted first Luke's sleeve and then Rosie's cloak.

"Where are your wristbands?"

"We don't have them because we are strangers."

"Hmm." The butcher took the necklace from Rosie and studied it carefully, remarking that it was not worth much.

"It's real gold," Rosie assured him. "Please, sir, please will you sell us some food?"

When Rosie pleaded with her grey eyes, she usually got her own way. Not today.

"Neither of you wear the emblem of the Guardians. You shall not buy from me," the butcher said firmly.

"Fair enough," said Luke reasonably. "Give the gold chain back to us, then."

The butcher put the necklace into his pocket. "What gold chain? I do not see a gold chain, do you?" he laughed.

"You can't do this!" Rosie exclaimed. "This is stealing! The chain belongs to our friend. Give it back now if you won't sell to us!"

Even as she spoke, two burly youths came to stand behind the butcher.

"These are my sons," the butcher said, and the young people knew that the words were meant as a threat, even though the butcher did not raise his voice.

Luke and Rosie were defeated. They walked away, pushing through the crowds. Rosie brushed the tears from her eyes. They had failed. Martha would be sad. Worst of all, they would still be hungry!

"We can't do anything about it," Luke told her as he led her away.

For a little while they wandered aimlessly around the market, not looking forward to returning to the farm with such bad news. Rosie's stomach growled. She was so hungry! Rosie may have been small but she had a healthy appetite. From the corner of her eye, she saw that on the stall nearest to them was a plate of meat pies, still warm. The smell made her mouth water. No-one would notice in this crowd if one or two pies went missing. In a moment, two pies were hidden under Rosie's cloak.

Before she could move, the Guardians had surrounded her. She heard a girl's voice shout, "It was that maiden! Arrest her! She is a thief and deserves punishment!"

Lindis had seen what had happened and seized her chance.

For what seemed like ages, but was actually only a moment, time stood still. The two girls faced each other, one dark-haired and dressed in fine silks, the other fair-haired and wearing peasant clothes.

Rosie knew Lindis served Lord Bellum. She had sensed it the first time they had met. Lindis hated Rosie and hated her friendship with Petroc. Now she could be rid of her.

Luke had seen what was happening. He also saw

the way in which Lindis looked at his sister. If he had liked Lindis in the past, he did not like her now.

"It wasn't Rosie, it was me," he said.

Lindis threw back her head and laughed spitefully. "The pies are still in her hand! Guards, arrest her, or my father shall hear that you have neglected your duty!"

One of the soldiers gave Luke a push so that he fell into the crowd. His last sight of Rosie was of a small, scared figure being led away between two very large Guardians.

As she was taken into the prison building, Rosie looked back over her shoulder to the place where she had last seen Luke. She had no time to see if he was still there, because she was pushed into a cell and left alone.

The room was small and bare, and Rosie sat on the bed, trembling and shaken by what had happened.

When she had time to think properly, she remembered how, when Lord Veritan had rested the golden sword of truth on them, he said that the sword represented the King's word and the King would give them power to stay true to this word. Rosie had failed. Instead of trusting the King to supply all her needs, she had taken matters into her own hands and tried to steal her food.

Meanwhile, Luke was running as fast as he could, back to the farm for help.

Chapter 12

"We must trust the King"

"Luke! Where is Rosie?" There was fear in Morwen's voice.

Petroc and Morwen had met Luke where the track from the village skirted the Dark Forest. Luke had spent his strength in his frantic race to get help. His chest hurt. He struggled to speak.

"What happened?" Petroc shouted impatiently.

Their faces turned white as Luke gasped out his story.

"I knew you should not have gone," Morwen wailed, for once shaken out of her usual composure. "I had a bad feeling about this. So did Petroc. That is why we came to meet you. How could you have let it happen, Luke?"

The accusation was unfair, but if Luke was looking for support from Petroc, he was to be disappointed.

"You mean they have locked Rosie away in their prison for taking two pies?" Petroc's voice shook with anger.

Luke nodded miserably. "I watched them take her away but I couldn't do anything to stop them!"

"Could not or would not?" Petroc shouted. "You could have done something, surely? You could have explained how hungry we all are!"

"Do you think that would make any difference?" Luke cried bitterly, his own anger rising at the unfairness of being blamed for something that was not his fault. "It was down to Lindis," he continued. "Lindis called the Guardians! She told them it was Rosie! Blame her!"

Petroc's eyes narrowed. "I do not believe you," he said flatly. "Lindis helped me when I was attacked. Why should she do this to us?"

"How do I know? And if I say it was Lindis, then it was Lindis. Don't you dare call me a liar! You weren't even there! How do you know what it was like?"

Luke and Petroc were shaping up for a fight and Morwen knew that she had to stop them.

"We must do something quickly," she said in her practical way. "Standing here arguing will not help Rosie. I feel we should return to the village."

Luke disagreed. "What good will that do? The Guardians will just quote their law to us and then refuse to let us see her. I know them."

"You do not know that for sure." Petroc was more reasonable now. "We have to try."

Luke, now fully recovered, said, "Maybe we should talk to the King first?"

So that was what they did, each one quietly asking the King to make a way for Rosie to be set free. The King always heard their thoughts, no matter where they were. Humbly, they asked for help in the name of Salvis, the King's son.

Almost at once they met Raldi, who was returning from the market with a basket of provisions. When he saw the young people, he stopped in his tracks and stared at them as though embarrassed. When he came nearer, they saw the reason for Raldi's dismay. On his wrist he wore the silver serpent. He had forsaken the King.

Raldi saw them looking at his hand. He could not meet Petroc's gaze.

"I have small children to feed. I could not bear to see them go hungry. It does not mean I serve Tomas. I am still loyal to the King in my heart."

"We do not judge you," Morwen said kindly, for who could blame a man for feeding his family?

Petroc added, "Are you really loyal to the King?"

"Of course I am. I still love the King. I believe the King understands our hardship and will be merciful."

That did not line up with what Veritan had told them. Veritan had said they should stay true to the King's word.

"We need your help." Petroc told him what had happened.

Raldi rubbed his beard. "Very well, I think I know what to do. That pie stall is owned by Mara, an old friend of your household, Petroc. Like me, she still loves the King. We must ask her to plead for the little maid."

"Even if this woman agrees, we cannot trust the Guardians, or anyone who is a part of them," Luke replied scornfully.

Raldi took a deep breath, well aware of Luke's meaning. "Now listen to me, boy. The Guardian law is just and fair. There is no reason why they should not free the maiden."

Luke decided to reserve judgement, but no-one could think of a better idea.

By the time they got back to the market place, the traders were packing up to go home.

"Mara is still here," Raldi told them. He took the plump, fair-haired woman to one side and for a long time they whispered together. Luke couldn't stop thinking about Rosie. She would be so afraid.

When Mara and Raldi returned, Mara was smiling.

"Petroc, Morwen, how are you?"

"Hungry," said Morwen honestly.

Petroc said nothing. He realised that Mara, yet another of their friends, had also accepted the silver serpent.

"Can you help us?" Luke interrupted. "We need to get my sister out of that place. Rosie isn't a thief!"

"She stole my pies," Mara pointed out. "However, Morwen, you were a good friend to me when my daughter was little. For that reason and for the love of Salvis that we share, I shall help you. Come with me."

The prison was on the other side of the market square, but it seemed to take for ever to get there. Mara pulled the bell cord, then Mara and Raldi went inside. They were gone for a long time.

"What can they be talking about?" Luke muttered anxiously.

"Setting Rosie free, I hope, brother," Petroc replied. Their argument was forgotten.

Morwen was again speaking to the King in her thoughts.

Then, quite suddenly and unexpectedly, it was all over! Rosie ran out to them. After a quick hug from Petroc and then Morwen, she threw herself into Luke's arms. She sobbed as if her heart was breaking.

"Mara has withdrawn her accusation," Raldi explained. "The Guardians had to accept her withdrawal."

"Thank you, Mara," Morwen said quietly.

The plump woman put her hand under Morwen's chin in a caring way. "Why not accept the silver serpent, child? You can still love and serve the King. Salvis was ever good and kind. He told us that the King is merciful and forgiving. Salvis would not expect you to live in this way."

The children recalled Lord Veritan's words again, and they thought of how much they loved Salvis.

"We must trust the King," Morwen whispered, trying to forget her hunger. It was very hard. If they did accept the serpent, surely that would not stop Salvis from loving them?

"No, we must trust the King," she repeated.

"Oh well, that is your decision, but I would not see my own children go hungry."

"Our mother would not want us to wear the serpent," Petroc replied, but not harshly, because Mara and Raldi were kindly people.

"I can still help you," Mara said. "I have my pony and cart. You may ride with me as far as your farm. It will save you the long walk home."

Rosie was suddenly very, very tired. Luke's face blurred in front of her, and she held tightly to him to save herself from falling over.

"Yes please," she sighed. "Oh yes, please."

When they waved goodbye to Mara and Raldi, Rosie felt unable to face the others and the questions they would ask.

"I need space," she explained. "That place was horrible. Can I go up High Hill a little way?"

"Only if I come with you," Petroc said firmly. "You are not to go alone."

As they began the climb, Petroc kept his arm around her shoulders. She still looked pale.

"Did they give you anything to eat?" he asked.

Rosie nodded. "Bread and cheese, but I'm still hungry. It hurts when I get so hungry. Do you feel like that? You never complain."

"I am well used to hunger," he sighed, and for a brief moment his green eyes betrayed painful memories.

"You mean when you were Carrik's prisoner?"

"And in Bellum's castle. If we displeased Bellum, we were not fed. We had to hunt for scraps under the tables after the others had finished eating. We had to crawl on the floor, like dogs... "

Petroc hardly ever spoke to anyone about that terrible time, but Rosie seemed to understand.

"You look tired, Rosie. Shall we rest?"

"I feel safe with you," she told him as they sat down on the soft grass. "I know nothing can hurt me when I'm with you."

Petroc remembered how he felt when she was in danger. "I'll never let anyone hurt you again, Rosie," he promised.

"We can see nearly all of the island from here," she said. "We can see the Dark Forest, the village, the Royal Palace... Oh, I could stay here always! I do love Karensa!"

Petroc shook his head in disbelief. "After today I would have thought you only wanted to go home?"

"I am home. I never want to go back to Cornwall... Petroc, I want to stay here with you... Petroc... "

"What is it?" Petroc could not understand how he could be so happy with so many troubles surrounding them, but each new problem increased the young people's love one for the other. Even Holly was not quite so bossy any more.

"Petroc, do you like me?"

He laughed. "Of course I do!"

"No, I mean do you really like me? More than the others?"

Petroc drew back a little. "Rosie, you are only twelve!"

"I won't be twelve for always. If... if I'm still here when I'm as old as Morwen, could we be close, like Morwen and Esram are close?"

Petroc looked at her. She was no longer a little girl. She was very pretty, with grey eyes and soft, fair hair, and she understood Petroc so well.

"Yes," he replied. "Yes, Rosie, if you are still here when you are older, we could become close like that... Rosie, don't cry again. The danger is past. You're safe now."

"I'm crying because I'm happy! Petroc, you're all I want in all the world. I'm never going home. I shall miss Dad and Stacey and Luke, if he goes home, but Karensa is where I belong. It's where Salvis lives, and I don't care about the danger and the hardships any more, just as long as we can be together one day."

Petroc brushed her hair, then her cheek with his hand. "Yes, Rosie, that is my desire too... But I fear you will be going home."

Chapter 13

Prisoners or guests?

Rosie and Petroc walked hand in hand from High Hill to the farm. Despite the hardships they faced, life was good. They had their friendship and for now, that was enough. All too soon they would face reality.

As they crossed the yard, something moved by the barn.

"You stay here. I shall see what it is," said Petroc, but Rosie ignored him and went to investigate.

"It's a goat!" Rosie squealed. "It's *our* goat come home!"

Petroc caught the animal before it could escape. "She really *is* our own goat!" he cried. "Look at the brown mark around her neck! She was waiting by the barn where she lived. I'm sure she knows us. She has to be our own goat."

"She is ours. Besides the brown mark, there's that streak down her back. Why should anyone go to the trouble to steal our goat and then bring her back again?"

"I don't know. Maybe she escaped? We must show the others!"

They led the goat right into the farmhouse. Martha was serving up a dish of thin vegetable soup which, with bread, was all they had for supper. Martha's mouth fell open when she saw the goat.

"I cannot believe my eyes!" she exclaimed. "She must have escaped from the people who stole her! Oh, this will help us to survive! We need her milk and cheese."

"I told you the King would bless you," Esram said, smiling.

During the next few weeks, the weather became steadily colder, for the Time of Snows was fast approaching. A daily supply of milk and cheese from the goat provided them with enough food to keep up their strength, even though the young people were still hungry.

One morning, when frost decorated the grass and hedges, Luke and Holly were stacking logs in the yard, the hard work warming them and making their cheeks rosy.

Luke and Holly were often together. Esram stayed with Morwen, learning farming ways. Rosie helped Martha in the kitchen. Petroc worked alongside Amos, in the fields or repairing the outbuildings. Today, Petroc had gone off alone, and Amos stood, lost in thought, just by the kitchen door.

As the weeks passed, Luke had discovered a different Holly. She might be bossy and opinionated, but she was also kind and understanding. She knew how it felt to lose her mother, and that formed a common bond between them. Luke's mother had died many years ago.

"I can't understand why I should feel so happy," Holly said. "Life is hard for us here. At home on the other side of the island, even with the Guardians in control, I had enough to eat."

"I don't think it is being happy," Luke replied

thoughtfully. "It's more like a sort of peace, inside. I know our life's hard, but Salvis is especially close to us now. Sometimes, after supper, when we sing our praise songs to the King, I almost expect to see him sitting with us."

"I never saw him again after that day in the barn. I'll never forget the night I asked the King to be part of my life and to forgive all the wrong things I've done. You and Rosie, you helped me. I wish I could see Salvis again. Really see him, I mean, standing next to me, not just feeling him near. Salvis is so... so..." Holly couldn't find the right words.

"Even if we can't see him, we know he's with us. That makes everything worthwhile."

Amos stood at the door, listening to them. How could he tell them there was no seed to plant for next year's harvest? Worse still, the taxes were soon due and their savings had been used to pay last month's taxes. Their money was gone.

Amos couldn't keep his secret for much longer. When the first sprinkling of snow covered the ground, he and Martha called everyone together around the kitchen table and told them how serious things were.

"Any day now, the Guardians will come for their money, and we have none," Martha explained.

"What shall we do?" Rosie watched flames from the fire leaping and dancing. She didn't want to hear this.

Amos looked very sad. "I fear they will claim the farm."

"No!" Petroc leapt to his feet and crashed his fist

on the table, startling everyone. "No, they will not have the farm! I will die first! This farm belonged to my father! I will not let it fall into Bellum's hands!"

Morwen was also deeply upset, but she was more realistic than her brother. "Uncle Amos, is there nothing we can do? Maybe they would accept one of us as a servant, instead of payment? If so, I am willing for them to take me!"

"They will not do that either!" her brother stormed.

Holly had the best idea. "Lindis used to be my friend. When we were little we played together. I would often go to Tomas' house for supper. If I went to Tomas now, I might soften his heart towards us."

Amos and Martha said no, emphatically, but Esram surprised everyone. He knew Holly better than the others knew her, and he thought she might succeed. She was bold enough. She could be determined to have her own way, as he had often found to his cost. Esram sensed that part of Lindis' cold heart still desired friendship.

"Holly should go," he said, and quietly and sensibly explained his reasons.

"She must not go alone then," said Amos. "I would need to go with her."

"Let's take a vote," Luke suggested. "All in favour, raise your hands."

Voting was quite new to them, but every hand was raised except one; Martha could not bring herself to send Amos and Holly into danger.

"Why then," said Holly brightly, "we must go

today and not wait any longer. Waiting makes us scared. We must get the thing over and done with."

"First, there is something we must do for you both," said Luke. He placed his hands on Holly. Petroc did the same for Amos, then they all asked the King to give special protection to their friends.

"Remember the golden sword," Luke whispered to Holly. "Salvis will be with you. Trust him, Holly. Just trust him." He held her hands for a moment, but she still looked unsure. They left within the hour.

Holly really was scared, but she would never admit it. Holly seldom revealed her true feelings.

"All will be well," Amos encouraged her. "We have the King's protection. And Tomas cannot punish us for this, surely?"

He spoke to reassure himself. Holly didn't answer and they continued through the Dark Forest in silence.

When they arrived at Tomas' house, it was swarming with Guardians. Amos and Holly were challenged as soon as they reached the door.

"We would see Tomas, your leader. We have urgent business." Amos sounded a great deal calmer than he felt.

"Who are you, peasants?" The guard's voice was scornful.

"I am Amos, a farmer, and this maiden is Holly, an old friend of Lindis, your leader's daughter."

"Who is it?" Lindis herself came to the door. She was as pretty as ever in a tunic of russet decorated with gold beads, her dark hair threaded with ribbons of gold. She always made Holly feel clumsy and plain.

"What do you want?" Lindis asked abruptly when she saw her visitor was Holly.

This was not going as well as she hoped. Holly had thought that maybe Lindis might take her visit as a gesture of friendship.

"We used to be best friends once? I thought you might help us. We need to speak with your father. Can you arrange that?"

Lindis folded her arms. Then she smiled. "I could do so, Holly, if I had a mind, but I have not forgotten how you pushed me in that pig pen. Why should I help you?"

"That was ages ago!" Holly cried. She gritted her teeth. It hurt to beg to Lindis. "Please help us, Lindis."

"I believe you forgot something when I came to the door? You must show me respect, Holly. The soldiers bow to me. You did not." She raised one delicate eyebrow as though waiting for them to obey.

Amos had no problem with this, but Holly had to take a deep breath and clench her fist before bowing her head.

"Oh, that was not very good!" Lindis cried.

Holly's knuckles dug into her hands as she bowed low. Her face was red with humiliation.

Lindis appeared to be satisfied. "That's much better. Now you can come in," she said.

She led them into a large, airy room where Tomas rested in a chair by the window. He was an impressive figure in his grey and blue uniform, a gold chain of office around his neck. His serpent bracelet was encrusted with jewels.

He seemed surprised to see them. "Holly? What are you still doing in these parts?"

Holly did not reply to his question. He probably knew the answer.

"We have come to ask a favour, sir," she said. Nervousness made her speak very fast. "This is Amos. I am staying on his farm. Or rather, his nephew Petroc's farm. Their taxes are due and they have no money to pay them."

"I see." Tomas rubbed his chin. The silver serpent sparkled as he moved his hand. "I see you do not wear the Guardians' mark, either of you?"

"No, we do not wear that, sir," said Amos. "We are the King's servants. We cannot wear the emblem that belongs to Lord Bellum."

Tomas laughed loudly, throwing back his head and slapping his knees with his hands.

"Your King does not provide well for his servants! You look half starved, your clothes are worn out and you have no money! That does not say much for your King! Accept the serpent and all your troubles will be over. You will trade freely and your taxes will be lowered. Holly, you are good at looking after your own interests. What do you say?"

"We cannot wear the serpent, sir," said Holly. "As for me, I have changed greatly."

Tomas would have thrown them out of the house, but Lindis whispered something in his ear and he changed his mind.

"Come here, Holly. Come close to me," he instructed.

Holly obeyed, looking scared. She stood by Tomas' chair and tried to stop her knees shaking. It was unreasonable to be afraid of someone she had known since she was a little girl.

"Holly, I could help you, but first you must help me. I am told that your father and that troublemaker, Carrik, are hiding in a secret place on the High Moor?"

"Are they?" Holly sensed danger.

"You know full well they are. Do not play games with me!" Tomas did not need to raise his voice to threaten her. "Holly, tell me where they are hiding and I will see that your taxes are paid."

Holly looked over her shoulder. Amos shook his head. He did not trust the Guardians to keep their word.

"No, sir," she replied. "I do not know where they are."

Tomas shrugged. "So be it. Those who cannot pay their taxes lose their land. I shall send men this day to claim your farm."

Their first thought was to get back home and warn the others, but before they could move, Tomas called his soldiers who stood between them and the door, their only means of escape.

"These people shall be our guests tonight," he said pleasantly. "Escort them to their room. Put them somewhere safe and see that they remain there."

Holly was furious. Anger overcame her fear. "You cannot do this! Your own law will not allow you to take prisoners without just cause!"

"Prisoners?" Tomas raised his eyebrows. "Did they say prisoners, Lindis?"

His daughter laughed. "They seem confused, Father. I always believed Holly was strange!"

"You are not prisoners," Tomas explained. "You are guests. You shall stay for supper. Who knows, Lord Bellum himself might call on us! Tomorrow morning, you shall go home. Only, by tomorrow you may not have a home to go to!"

Chapter 14

A kind of madness

Petroc tried to keep the day as normal as he could, but it was impossible. Everyone could only think of Amos and Holly. He gave up and asked Rosie to come for a walk. They linked their arms to keep warm.

"Some lambs should be ready for slaughter in a few months," Petroc remarked, surveying his flock. Then he laughed at her horrified expression. "If you are going to stay on Karensa, you will have to grow used to such things."

"I am going to stay. I've made up my mind. I shall learn to do everything on the farm, just like you. You must teach me."

"Did you mean it, then?"

"Of course. If I'm to live here, I shall do farm work."

"We might not have a farm for much longer!"

"Do I mean more to you than your farm?" she asked, mischievously.

"Yes." He was quite serious. "You are more important to me than the farm."

"More than the King?"

"No, not more than the King."

She seemed pleased. "That's as it should be. All is well with us, I feel... There, I am speaking in the island way."

Without warning, the peace in Petroc's heart was

broken. "We should return to the farm. We should go back now," he said urgently. Rosie trusted him completely and didn't argue. They left at once, but even so, by the time they reached the farm, the Guardians had arrived.

Petroc took command, with Luke and Esram standing firmly behind him. They had sent the girls inside.

"What is your business on my farm?" Petroc demanded. He drew himself up to his full height and stood proudly.

The leader was a well-built, stocky man with a broad, country accent, who may once have been a farmer himself.

"Our business, young master, is your tax to the Guardians which is unpaid. We have come to collect it."

"We cannot pay you at this moment. My uncle has gone to see Tomas to resolve the problem."

The leader inclined his head. "We have come from Tomas. The matter was not resolved. Tomas has instructed us to take your farm, which is now the property of the Guardians. You have six days to pack your belongings and find somewhere else to live. Tomas is not unreasonable. Until the six days are gone, we must show that the farm is now Guardian property. We have come to paint our sign on each of your walls, so that people will know it is ours."

They dismounted, tethered their horses to the farm fence and took brushes and paint from their saddlebags. The leader issued instructions.

"Paint this wall first! Make the emblem large enough to be seen by any who pass by!"

A kind of madness came upon Petroc as he watched the first man begin to paint a black serpent on the farmhouse wall.

"You shall not do this!" Petroc yelled, and with a strength greater than his own strength, he knocked paint and brush from the soldier's hands. The Guardian, taken completely by surprise, allowed the boy to get the better of him.

With that single movement, all the children's pent up feelings, all their hardship and hunger, exploded. Esram and Luke joined Petroc in his fight. They seized the paint and threw it at the Guardians, shouting and laughing as the soldiers were covered in black paint.

They were joined by Rosie and Morwen, who threw whatever they could lay their hands on, pelting the soldiers with clods of earth, rotting vegetables, even dung. Anything they could find was thrown.

Rosie stood close to Petroc. She was scooping mud in her hands and throwing it in every direction. Luke and Esram had taken logs from the wood pile. These hurt when they hit their target, and soldiers were jumping up and down, rubbing their arms and shins.

Paint was everywhere. Morwen was heard screaming at the Guardians to go home. Rosie was laughing. Esram stopped throwing logs and took paint and brush to blot the serpent from the wall. Luke was swirling paint in every direction and singing loudly, though he didn't know why! Hens were clucking and running round in circles, scared silly by the turmoil.

Martha stood at the farmhouse door, her hands

raised in horror, crying for them to stop. They didn't even hear her.

All too soon, the Guardians recovered and the leader regained control, swearing as he brushed paint and dung from his clothes.

"Seize the red-headed boy! He is the ringleader! Take him and leave the others! We shall make an example of that one!"

Petroc did not give them time to seize him. The soldiers' horses were waiting patiently. In a red haze of anger, Petroc untied the nearest horse and leapt on its back. Grabbing the axe from the wood pile, he rode off at breakneck speed into the Dark Forest, flourishing the axe and shouting that no-one would ever take his farm.

Filled with this strange madness, Petroc rode recklessly, careless that the horse might stumble on a tree root. Dark trees and thorny bushes sped past him and he did not see them. His one thought was to reach the fisher village and when he got there, he knew exactly what to do. The Guardians, more cautious, were unable to catch him.

Once through the Dark Forest, Petroc turned and rode into the village. Women screamed and pulled their children out of the way as he hurtled through the narrow streets, still brandishing the axe. He stopped in front of the new prison.

"We will not have you Guardians here!" he yelled, swinging the axe around his head in a mad frenzy.

"You shall not make prisoners of the King's people!" he shouted, and began to hack at the heavy wooden door.

He felt a sharp pain on the back of his head and before he could tell who had hit him, he fell to the ground and his world of red anger became silent and black.

Petroc forced his eyes open, resisting the pain of daylight. He knew at once that he was in a cell. Prison had a smell unlike any other. He remembered it from Lord Bellum's castle.

"You are back with us, then?"

Petroc groaned as he moved his head and for a moment, the blackness returned. When he opened his eyes again, he was lying on a narrow bed in a small, light room with bars at the window. A guard had been left with him. They were taking no chances, for this man was twice Petroc's size and fully armed. Petroc noticed that the room was spotlessly clean.

Such a thought at such a time, was so ridiculous that he almost laughed.

"Get up," the guard commanded. "Come, lad, I have to attend that wound."

He seemed kind, even if he was a Guardian. He helped the boy to sit up and produced a basin of warm water and a cloth.

His hands were surprisingly gentle as he cleaned the wound. "It is not too bad. You must have a thick head, boy. You will not even need a bandage. Now, wash your face and tidy up."

"Why?" Petroc said thickly, feeling dizzy again. "I'm not going anywhere, am I? You are not going to set me free?"

"No, you will not go free," the guard said sadly. He was a kind man who had sons of his own. He could imagine that if they had been there, his boys might have been throwing paint with the rest of them. He felt sorry for this boy. Tomas was going to make an example of him. If the decision had been left to the guard, Petroc would have received a sound beating and been sent to bed with no supper.

"You will not go free, boy. Tomas and his leaders are on their way now. Your trial will be held here because Tomas is determined that a verdict will be reached this night."

Chapter 15

"I will never leave you"

Luke stood outside the prison door. Even with Esram at his side, he was nervous. Just as Petroc's axe had made little impression on the thick, iron-bound door, so his rebellion had made little impression on the Guardians.

The news of Petroc's arrest and of his strange trial, was quickly spreading to the village and farms. Tomas had appointed himself as judge and had passed sentence, and most people believed that Petroc deserved punishment. The Guardians looked after them far better than the King had ever done. No-one ever went hungry. The sick were cared for. If Petroc's family were penalised, it was their own fault for refusing to accept the silver serpent.

"Only one visitor is allowed," the soldier who answered the door told them abruptly.

"You should be the one to see him," said Esram. "Petroc was your friend before he was mine. I shall wait outside."

Luke did not argue, so Esram went to sit on a low wall outside. He closed his eyes and tried to speak to Salvis but the words wouldn't come. His thoughts were muddled.

"What is happening?" A voice interrupted him. Lindis was shaking his shoulder with one hand and holding her pony with the other.

Esram wasn't deceived by her concern. "Petroc is in prison. He rebelled against the Guardians. He has been tried by your father and will be punished tomorrow. I have asked Salvis to help him. The King loves him, just as he loves each one of us, even you, Lindis, if you would only turn to him and ask him to forgive you."

Lindis blanched. "So that was where my father went tonight! You say Petroc will be punished? What will happen to him?"

"I don't know. They are saying he is a traitor."

With a strangled gasp, Lindis mounted up and rode away as fast as she could. First she must get home, then she must go to Lord Bellum's castle, across the Meadow of Flowers.

Petroc gave a shaky grin. "I've done it now, haven't I?"

"What have they decided?" Luke did not return the smile.

"Oh, that I am a traitor and will receive the punishment for treason tomorrow morning. They say there is no place for traitors on Karensa."

"That's the most ridiculous thing I ever heard!"

"That's what they say I am."

"What will they do?"

"Probably a beating." Petroc avoided his friend's eyes. "I have received worse in the past. They might send me back to Bellum's castle."

"You're only fifteen! They won't be too harsh with you! And we won't let them send you back to Bellum's castle!"

Even as the words were spoken, he remembered that Esram had only been fourteen when the

Guardians had wanted to set him adrift to drown.

Fear gripped Luke's heart. Fear not for himself, but for Petroc. Unspeakable fear.

He stared at his friend, not knowing what to say.

"Luke... will you do something for me?"

"Anything," he promised.

"Will you... if I should... if it should be something really terrible, like... like... will you comfort Rosie and Holly and... and my mother?"

Luke nodded, too overcome to speak.

"And Luke... ask... ask Esram to take care of Morwen and to look after my farm?"

Luke found his voice. "Don't talk like this, Petroc! Don't speak as though we shan't see each other again! We'll help you to escape! Don't worry, we'll never let them take you back to Bellum! We'll rescue you! You could come back to Cornwall with us! You would be safe there!" He was speaking wildly now. "I'll go to the Royal Palace and get Salvis. He won't leave you now. He won't let—"

"Luke!" Petroc placed his fingers over Luke's mouth. "We don't have time for such foolish talk. There are things I must say to you... Luke, you have been the best friend I could ever have. Better than a brother to me."

"Don't talk like this!"

"No, let me finish. I want to remember the good times. The first time I saw you, I'd so needed a friend and then you came to the farm and glared at us as though you hated everyone!"

"I don't hate you!" Luke choked on his words. "Petroc, I never had a friend like you! We shall find Amos and have you set free. We—"

Before he could finish what he was saying, a guard returned and ushered him away. The boys did not even have time to say goodbye to each other and there was desperation in Luke's eyes as the cell door slammed shut.

When Luke had gone, Petroc had no more need to hide his fear. Trembling, he leant back against the wall of the cell and slid to the floor. The punishment for treason was death. Tomas had told him that in the morning he was going to die.

"Salvis! Salvis, where are you? Help me! Help me now, please! I need you so! I never needed you like I do tonight! Help me, please! Make me strong! I don't want to die! Take the fear away! Salvis, don't leave me on my own!"

The room was silent. Salvis seemed to have deserted him.

It was the guard, his enemy, who stayed with him that night, so that he would not be alone.

Esram and Luke stood outside the prison, which was now heavily guarded in case of trouble. Esram could tell by Luke's face that the news was bad. Briefly, Luke explained what was going to happen.

"We can't let them beat him! And Petroc won't survive in Bellum's castle a second time. What shall we do?" Luke asked.

"Maybe we should go back to the farm? The girls are on their own. I do not know if Amos and Holly are back yet. Amos would know what to do."

"You go. I can't leave Petroc alone, even if I only stand here, I can't just leave him! And we don't need to worry about the girls. Look!"

Morwen and Rosie ran to them, hot and out of breath from their long journey.

"They found Petroc guilty of treason," Luke told them. "He will be beaten tomorrow morning, in the square."

Rosie gasped. "They can't do that to him! We won't let them! It's against the law!"

"This is Karensa, not home," her brother reminded her.

"We have to get him free," Rosie cried. "Luke, think of something. What shall we do?"

"I don't know!" he shouted. "Why ask me?" Then he remembered what he had just promised Petroc. "Rosie, what can we do? How can we help him?"

"Look at the guards," Esram added. "They are standing three deep around the prison. They don't intend him to escape."

Morwen put her arm around Rosie. "We cannot free him now. Our only hope is to rescue him tomorrow when he is led out to the square." She looked doubtfully at Esram. "What do you think?"

"It might work," he replied slowly. "If we had horses. Or better still, a cart. Maybe we could push through and escape to the moors. I know where my uncle is hiding. No-one would find us there."

"It's worth a try," Luke said. "We can't just leave him, can we? Esram, we should be able to find a cart?"

"You go," said Morwen. "Rosie and me, we'll stay here, just to be near him. We can ask Salvis to send help."

No-one had a better idea, so the boys went off together, leaving Morwen and Rosie to keep a vigil outside the prison until morning.

Petroc saw the crowd and took an involuntary step back as cold terror gripped his heart. He looked at his guard, the one who had been kind to him.

"Will it... will it hurt very much?"

The man shook his head. He had no stomach for this work. He knew that Tomas was trying to scare the lad into submission, but this was cruel.

"It will not hurt for long. But this need not happen! You can still change your mind and accept Guardian rule. You are not yet sixteen, boy! That is so young! Be wise! Take your freedom. You can still serve your King."

He was led out between the soldiers and the waiting crowd murmured quietly. The people here were used to serving the King, who was just and merciful. They were not sure they approved of punishing people in this way.

The soldiers had tied Petroc's hands, so his guard helped him onto the platform, where the leader of the Guardians was waiting.

Tomas spoke loudly, so that everyone could hear.

"Petroc, you have been found guilty of treason. Guardian law does not usually inflict the ultimate penalty, but treason is an exception. There is no place on Karensa for traitors. Yet even now, if you ask for mercy and accept the silver serpent, you will go free. You will be home tonight, and you will not lose your farm."

Petroc looked across the village square. The sun was rising and frost sparkled in the morning light. Beyond the village was the sea, and in the other direction, the Dark Forest, High Hill and his farm.

111

Petroc loved Karensa. He wanted desperately to go free.

"My hands are tied," he replied.

He was not speaking of the ropes binding him, but of his great love for the King which would not let him go. To give in now would mean that all he had lived for was worthless. He pictured the golden sword of truth, its blade shining so brightly that none could look upon it.

Tomas told him to kneel on some straw in the centre of the platform and once again, the guard helped him.

Now that the time had come, Petroc was more sad than he was afraid.

Sad for so many years he would never see, for lost sunsets and unexplored dawns; sad that he would never walk through the Dark Forest, nor breathe the cool morning air.

Sad that he would never watch the dolphins playing in the surf or feel the soft sand beneath his feet; sad that he would never climb High Hill and survey his farm, the work of his hands; sad for harvests he would not reap and for fruit he would not gather.

Sad that he would never grow to be a man; sad that he would never have children of his own.

He felt a gentle touch on his shoulder and realised that he did not kneel alone.

Salvis smiled and his brown eyes were so full of compassion that Petroc's face was transformed by joy. The Lord he had served had promised never to leave him. Salvis would not let him die alone.

Tomas lifted his sword. Petroc, his eyes fixed firmly on Salvis, never saw it fall.

Chapter 16

Destiny

Rosie fainted. Morwen stood as though carved from stone, her face ashen and her hands held over her mouth to stifle the scream in her heart.

Luke and Esram abandoned the cart they had been trying to drive through the crowd, and ran towards the girls, scared there might be reprisals against them.

For a moment there was silence, then a strange sound came from the watching crowd, a low muttering of discontent. No-one had expected Tomas to take Petroc's life, no matter what he had done.

Turmoil broke out as Lord Bellum's black horse hurtled into the square, followed by Lindis on her pony. The crowd moved back in fear of the Lord of Darkness.

"Stop!" Bellum screamed. "Stop! Do not touch that boy!"

But he was too late. He leapt from his horse and up to the platform. Holding his hands high, his face contorted with rage, he roared like an angry lion.

"What have you done? What have you done?"

Tomas was bewildered. He had thought it would please his master to be rid of this adversary.

"But, lord... this boy was nothing but trouble... He was your enemy... he hated you... "

"I wanted him to come back to me! He would

113

have come back to me! The maiden would have persuaded him to come back, in time! Now it is too late! Now he is out of my reach for ever! You have lost the battle for me! Get out of my sight and take your daughter with you!"

Lindis began to cry. "What have I done, master? I set Holly and Amos free, so they could rescue him! I came to warn you! You promised Petroc would be mine! What have I done that you should punish me?"

"You are your father's daughter. That is your crime," Lord Bellum growled. "Both of you, go from my sight until I decide your fate."

Salvis looked exactly as Petroc remembered him, tall and slim, his brown hair parted in the centre and falling loosely around his oval face. His dark eyes were full of love. In his presence nothing seemed to matter, except this great and wonderful love.

Petroc and Salvis looked back to the chaos they were leaving behind. Petroc saw Rosie lying at Morwen's feet and he longed to go back for them, but Salvis shook his head.

"Others will take care of them, Petroc. You have to leave them now and come with me."

In no time at all they had travelled through the Dark Forest to the place where the Royal Palace stood in all its magnificence. Its silver pennants and golden turrets shone in the cold morning sunlight.

"This will now be your home," Salvis explained.

Petroc could not resist turning his head to look at the Dark Forest again. A deer peeped from a thicket.

"Do not look back," said Salvis. "Your work on Karensa is finished. All your struggles are over, and you have accomplished all things well. My father the King is waiting to greet you. Now you will start a new life, the life that was destined to be yours since days before time."

When he and Rosie had gone for a walk together, Petroc had no idea he was going to die. Now it was over and there was nothing left to fear any more. The guard had been right. The sword had not hurt. Or perhaps he had forgotten the pain?

"Salvis, last night... I called for you and you didn't answer. Why didn't you help me? I was so alone."

"You were not alone. I was there, and the guard was with you."

"But he was my enemy! He was kind, but he's a Guardian!"

"Not for much longer. Already this man's heart is turned towards the King. He will be changed."

Petroc was pleased. He had liked the guard. "But why didn't you come yourself, Lord?"

"You needed to make the final decision," Salvis explained. "I could not make the choice for you. The ache in your heart will soon be forgotten. In my father's Palace there is no sadness, no tears, no pain. There is only laughter and peace and joy. You will see for yourself. Come with me."

Petroc had been to the Royal Palace once before, in the days when it was still possible for people to go to the King each evening at the Time of Decisions, but the Palace was never as splendid as this!

They entered the Great Hall, and it was beautiful

beyond all imagination! The Three Thrones on a high dais with marble steps, the changing lights of silver, rose and gold, the wonderful music!

Music was everywhere. On either side of the Hall, the King's servants stood clothed in shining white, singing praises in words older than time and sweeter than tomorrow's dawn; secret words of ancient days; words that Petroc had received long ago when he gave his heart to the King, only now the words were not secret any more. He understood them as easily as the language of his birth.

As they moved towards the Three Thrones, every servant bowed the knee. Petroc supposed they were kneeling to Salvis, but when he looked round, Salvis was no longer with him. He walked alone. He could not imagine why the King's servants should kneel to him. He was no-one important, only a poor farmer's son. He was not rich or famous.

Before he reached the thrones, a man approached him. "Petroc! Welcome home!"

At first Petroc did not recognise the man. Then he did. "Father! Oh, I've missed you!"

Tobias laughed with joy as he held out a father's arms to embrace his son. Tobias looked so well! His back was straight and he walked tall.

"Come, Petroc. Come with me."

His father led him forward, then stepped away as they reached the Three Thrones. Petroc must climb the steps alone. He was not afraid, for he trusted Salvis.

Petroc looked at the King's face, which was bathed in a strange silver light. He was just as

Petroc had remembered him, his face neither young nor old, despite his grey hair and beard. The jewels from his crown were reflected in his royal robes of purple and gold.

To the left of the King sat the Unseen Lord, who gave power to the King's people. His throne was surrounded by light the colour of a rose sunset.

But on the right hand side of the King, Salvis was now in golden glory. He was no longer a peasant. His face shone brighter than the sun, his robes were dazzling white and he wore a crown surrounded by moving light. His eyes blazed fire, but when Petroc dared to look at his face, he saw that this Wonderful Being was the same Salvis he had loved and served.

Salvis spoke to his Father. "Lord King, I bring you Petroc, son of Tobias. He has accepted me as Lord and has been your faithful servant, sacrificing his life rather than deny you."

"Petroc, you are welcome." The King's voice was still mighty. "There are many wonders for you to see in my Palace, many new and exciting things for you to do. But first, you must accept your reward. Well done. You have been a good and faithful servant. Receive your crown."

Lord Veritan came forward carrying a white robe. The King placed a diadem of light over Petroc's red hair and Veritan draped the robe over his shoulders and as he did this, Petroc's appearance became shining white from head to toe.

So Petroc knelt before the King's throne and he worshipped him in freedom and joy, and he knew peace and love beyond his dreams. This was his destiny.

One day, Salvis would ride out from the Royal Palace, followed by his army of loyal servants, and then Bellum would receive his just punishment for disobeying the King.

On that day, Salvis would claim back Karensa for his Father. On that day, all things would come right and be as they were created to be.

On that day, wickedness would end, and Bellum's power would be over. Then the people of Karensa would again enjoy free and true fellowship with their King.

As Petroc's voice rose in praise, his trials and hardships faded away. In the radiance of the King's Presence, he found love and joy and fulfilment and peace. For this he was created and everything that had happened to him, good or bad, became less than a thought on the breeze.

Chapter 17

A name that is higher

"We must get to them! We don't know what Tomas might do next!" Esram gasped as he and Luke fought their way through to Morwen and Rosie.

Luke saw his sister lying white and still, and Morwen, who seemed to be carved from stone. He wanted to help them, but he was so shocked that he couldn't move.

"Petroc's dead," was all he could say, and he repeated the words over and over again.

It was Mara, the pie stall owner, who saved them. Mara had given Esram and Luke her cart, but the two boys had been unable to push through the throng on the market square. They had been forced to abandon it at the side of the road.

Mara elbowed her way through. "Get the maidens on the cart! Escape to the moors!"

Luke was still muttering, "Petroc's dead... "

Esram gave him a shake. "We could be dead too if we don't get away from here. You bring Morwen. I'll carry Rosie."

"No, Rosie's my sister!" Luke moved at last and bent down to scoop her up in his arms. She was small and light and easy to carry. Esram half pushed, half dragged Morwen along, thankful that the cart was still where they had left it.

"Hurry!" Mara urged. "I cannot believe what

Tomas has done this day!" She was sobbing. "Go, children. Escape while you may, and the King's blessing go with you!"

Esram drove while Luke cradled Rosie's head on his lap and also steadied Morwen, who still had not said a word. She was breathing in short gasps and looked as though she would fall over at any moment.

As they hurtled away, they saw Amos and Holly running towards the market square.

"We cannot stop!" cried Esram. "There is no time. The Guardians have killed Petroc. Tomas might plan to punish Morwen, too."

Holly's scream resounded around the square. Amos stared in disbelief. Bellum was pacing across the platform, his hands tearing at his own hair in anger. Lindis was sobbing. Tomas stood alone and confused, not knowing which way to turn. The Guardians were unsure, their hands hovering over their swords. What did Lord Bellum expect them to do? The crowd's discontent grew. Only Bellum's presence held them back.

Holly stopped screaming and burst into tears. Petroc had never hurt anyone! He was always kind. How could they do this to him? Holly felt as though her heart was being torn apart.

Amos had loved Petroc like a son. He asked Bellum if he could take the boy home, but Bellum was too angry to hear him, so Amos quietly and gently lifted Petroc from the platform. With Holly following behind, he carried him away. The crowd parted respectfully to make a passage.

Bellum gave one last, dreadful cry then mounted his black horse and rode away.

At first, the crowd was silent, then suddenly, one man moved. Raldi leapt onto the platform. Pushing the Guardians to one side and ignoring their drawn swords, he held out his arm wearing the serpent bracelet.

"Get the key and unlock this thing! I will no longer wear this emblem!"

Bellum's departure helped the people to overcome their fear, and many followed Raldi. Very soon, Tomas was surrounded. He must order his soldiers to arrest everyone, or he must give in; there were so many of them.

He handed the keys to Raldi. With shouts of triumph, the people renounced the emblem of Bellum's authority as they threw the silver serpents on the blood-soaked straw where Petroc had died.

"We will have no more of this government!" Raldi shouted, and was supported by a loud cheer from the people.

"We will go back to the days of the King's rule!"

Esram drove the cart through the Dark Forest, avoiding Tomas' house and crossing the ford where they had all met on the day Luke and Rosie had arrived. It was a long journey, and although Esram drove the horse as fast as he dared, it was some time before they began to climb to the High Moors.

When they reached an open plateau, he stopped the cart, because the horse was exhausted. Esram shivered. It was bitterly cold. Already the heather clad moors were white with the first snow.

"How are the girls?" he asked anxiously.

"Still shocked," Luke replied. Rosie was drifting in and out of consciousness. Morwen sat holding to the side of the cart and staring straight ahead. Her face was expressionless.

"We will not stop long, but we have to rest the horse. We must get away from Bellum. He will hate us even more now that Petroc is... is... "

"Dead!" Morwen spoke the word for him. "Petroc is dead!" She gave a deep cry and burst into tears. Esram swung over to the back of the cart and took her in his arms.

Luke remembered how once before he had comforted Morwen. Now it was Esram she turned to.

"He knew last night he was going to die, but he never told me," said Luke. "Esram, he asked you to look after the farm."

Esram nodded as if that was what he would expect to do. "First we must reach safety," he said.

It was too late. A horseman was approaching. That black horse belonged to Lord Bellum!

The Lord of Darkness stopped in front of the cart so that it was impossible for them to pass. His face was pale. His eyes flickered with amber, a sure sign of rage. His hair was tangled where he had pulled at it with his bare hands and his clothes were dirty and torn.

"You children have been nothing but trouble!" he hissed. "I should have put an end to you long ago."

Luke was so consumed by grief that he was no longer scared of Bellum's threats.

"Why didn't you, then? I'll tell you why! If you kill us, you'll never be able to get us in your castle, that's why! Well, you're wasting your time! You'll never get Petroc, now! None of us will ever join you! Do the worst you can to us, Bellum. We don't care!"

Bellum's eyes narrowed and he leant forward on his horse. "Oh, you will care, Luke! Do you think that because you come from the lands beyond the mist, that will save you? It will not! I have the power to ruin each and every thing you set your heart upon."

Luke faced him squarely. "You have no power over me except the power I allow you to take, and that's no power at all. There's a Name that is higher than your name, higher than any other name. In that Name I command you to leave us alone!"

Luke never knew where he found the words. Energy surged through his spirit.

To their astonishment, Lord Bellum dismounted and, very briefly, bowed his knee. Then he mounted his black horse and without another word, rode away.

"How did you do that?" Esram gasped.

Luke had even surprised himself. "I don't know! It wasn't me! I just... the words just came out of my mouth!"

Morwen's sobs had subsided a little and Esram handed her back to Luke.

"We had better go."

"I think we should turn back," said Luke. "I don't think Bellum will trouble us any more. At least, not for a while."

Esram agreed and they turned the cart around, but not before they caught sight of a small, bedraggled figure struggling across the moor. Lindis was on her way home.

So they went home to the farm and arrived just as Amos, Raldi and Holly returned with Petroc's body. Martha's scream aroused Rosie. Her heart was broken and her dreams were shattered. Rosie wept as she had never wept before.

That night, Holly stayed with her and comforted her. Once, long ago, when Holly's heart was breaking, Rosie had stayed with her.

When Petroc was laid to rest by his father's side, it was snowing, just as it had snowed the day Tobias died. Shortly after the burial, Veritan arrived. This great Lord of the Palace knelt in silence and placed the golden sword of truth on Petroc's resting place.

"I honour a true heart," Veritan said. "Petroc gave his life rather than deny the King's word. I salute him." Then he lifted up the golden sword and rode away, leaving them to share their grief.

Amos fell to his knees, tired and full of sorrow. Esram supported Martha. Petroc's mother didn't cry, but she seemed all at once very old and very tired.

"First my dear husband, now my beloved son," she said, and although her voice shook with her terrible sorrow, there was no bitterness in her. "Oh, Petroc, why you? My own dear son, part of me has died with you!"

"I shall look after you," Esram promised.

Snow drifted down thick and fast as one by one their friends and neighbours came to say goodbye to Petroc. The silver serpents were gone from their wrists.

They stood in silence. There was no need for words. Petroc would never be forgotten.

Chapter 18

"I shall still praise the King!"

Rosie stood alone by Petroc's grave. Her heart ached so much! Luke found her, shivering in the dark, and he comforted her as best he could.

"I was going to stay on Karensa," she whispered between deep sobs. "I was never going back to Cornwall. I couldn't leave Petroc."

Luke searched for the right words. "I know, Rosie, but in time the pain won't be as terrible as it is today. I still miss Mum, but it doesn't hurt like it used to when she first died. Rosie, we shall never forget Petroc. We shall always be sad that he died. But it won't hurt like it does today. And Rosie... you're not the only one to miss him!" And then Luke cried, too, and it was his own tears that helped her.

"His face when he died!" Rosie whispered. "Luke, he looked full of joy, as though... as though he'd seen Salvis."

"Salvis wouldn't leave him to face the sword alone. I believe he was by his side, at the end."

After a while, Martha came to see where they were and took them inside to the warmth of the fire. That night they both slept soundly, for they were exhausted.

The following morning, Raldi called his friends and together they went to see Tomas, and told him plainly that they would no longer accept the Guardians as their rulers. They would go back to the old laws of the King. A government that was so cruel was not a government they desired.

"The boy was a traitor," Tomas protested. "He was nothing but trouble to everyone. He rebelled against the Guardians' right judgement and he led others to do the same. The punishment for treason is death. Petroc deserved to die."

"No," Raldi said calmly. "Petroc did not deserve to die. He was not a traitor. He was a young man who remained loyal to his rightful King and who was persecuted by your Guardians until he could endure no more. He fought for his family. He loved the King. We had forsaken that love in our concern for our own comfort. Petroc has shamed us. We shall be asking the King to forgive us and restore us. We want no more of you or your Guardians! We have removed our wristbands. You may keep them. And Petroc's family shall keep their farm. You shall not touch them. Neither is this house yours. It belongs to Carrik, who is one of us."

That was a long speech for Raldi, who was usually a man of few words. When he had finished talking, those he had brought with him applauded.

Tomas had to accept their decision, and Raldi and his friends walked from Carrik's house unharmed and free.

Bellum, splendid in purple velvet, his dignity restored, strode into Tomas' house. The anger he had displayed at Petroc's death still brooded over him.

"Where is the girl?" he demanded.

Tomas fell on his face. "Lindis has been captured, lord. My men found her on the High Moor, trying to escape. They brought her back here and she is now under lock and key."

"Bring her to me!"

Tomas scrambled to his feet and sent servants scurrying to obey him. They brought in Lindis, and Bellum's lip curled. Her clothes were stained with mud and her lovely hair was dirty and tangled. Her face was bruised and streaked with tears. She stood shaking before her master.

"How dare you stand in my presence?" Bellum thundered and, together with Tomas, Lindis threw herself to the floor.

Bellum look upon them with loathing. "I have come here to decide what to you with you both! No-one could blame me if I had you killed! Death is what you deserve! All this time I have worked and planned to get that boy back into my castle and you have snatched him from me! Because of your stupidity, the people have turned against the Guardians and removed the silver serpents from their wrists."

"I tried to stop it, master!" Lindis whined. "I came to fetch you!"

"Yes, you did. You put your duty to me above your duty to your father, but the punishment cannot be his alone. You will both return to the far side of the island. Tomas, you will hand over leadership of the Guardians to another of my choice. Your new master shall have your house on the far side of the island. You must earn your living by the work of your own hands. Be thankful for my mercy!"

He strode away and with the speed of the west wind, he rode back to his castle beyond the Meadow of Flowers.

Tomas stood to his feet and glared at his daughter. He lived for power. It meant more than anything to him, more than riches, more even than his own family. Now, that power had been taken away from him.

"Daughter, you betrayed me in trying to keep the boy from being punished. You failed, but you will no longer be free to cause mischief. From now on, you will stay within whatever walls we shall call our home. Your home will be your prison. Servants, remove her. The sight of her offends me!"

The next morning, Tomas, Lindis and the Guardians packed their belongings and departed back to the far side of the island.

When they heard that the Guardians had gone home, Amos called a special meeting at the farm. It had been so long since they had been free to praise the King together.

Before the meeting began, Raldi stepped forward and asked if anyone wished to speak about Petroc.

"I will be the first," he said. "Petroc was true and loyal to the King and a good friend to me."

A man called Daris stepped forward. "Many years ago, a storm damaged my fences and Petroc helped me mend them. He could only have been ten years old at the time. He did not leave his chores to help me, but came in his own time after his father's work was finished."

A woman followed him. "Bellum's men seized my goods because I could not pay my rent. Petroc spoke up for me. He was a prisoner himself and was punished for trying to help me."

One by one, people went forward. Luke's heart was thumping. He knew that he had to speak. He went to the front.

"Petroc was my brother in all but blood," he declared. "He once saved me from being captured, by surrendering himself. I shall never forget him."

After that, Raldi called for any who had deserted the King to ask for his forgiveness and commit their lives afresh. He was the first to do this, and many others responded.

Then they sang, their voices louder and louder, their hands held high in praise.

Luke and Rosie stood near the back. Rosie's tears were gone. She had found it very difficult to praise the King tonight because all she could think of was Petroc. When she closed her eyes, she saw him die, over and over again. Yet when she did begin to worship, she knew that Salvis was with her in a way she had never felt before.

Luke's heart was heavy. Although he tried his best, the songs were just words because praise refused to spring from his heart. He sat down, and buried his face in his hands.

"Salvis, why did you take Petroc away? First my mum, now my best friend! Why did Petroc have to die? He... he shouldn't be out in the cold... lying in the ground... he ought to be in here, with us. I don't want him to be dead! I want to talk to him again! I don't want this to have happened! Salvis, where are you? I need you!"

At that moment, Morwen walked to the front of the meeting and whispered to Raldi, who put his arm around her to encourage her.

"This is a sad time for all of us," she began. "I feel Salvis wants to comfort us, if only we will let him." Her voice wavered. "I am sad," she admitted. "Oh, please ask the King to help me!"

"This family needs us," Raldi declared. "All of you, come to the front! Luke and Rosie, you come too. You are now part of this household."

Martha held out her hand to Rosie, who was unsure.

"All will be well," she told her.

And it was well. They stood together, holding hands while everyone asked the King to comfort them and bring them peace.

"Oh, he's here!" Rosie breathed. "Salvis is really here. I can feel his peace going into my heart!"

"So can I," said Luke, and was sorry for his unbelief.

Before they returned to their places, Esram had something to say.

"I believe that the King is asking me to bring a message to you. I believe the King is telling us that what we have endured is only the beginning. Others will give their lives before Salvis returns to claim Karensa again. The King wants to prepare us! He says he is going to help us and that we are not to be afraid." He turned to Morwen. "The King has a special word for you, Morwen. He is saying that now your real work will begin. The King is going to allow you to see visions of things to come and at times Salvis will speak his own desires into your heart in a way that will enable you to help others."

A thought came to Luke. It was not his own thought. He took a deep breath because he had never done this before.

"The King is saying that this farm was saved for his purpose. On the far side of the island, people are being punished for their loyalty to the King, just as we have been punished here. Many children will need a safe haven. This farm is to be a refuge for those in need and all must be made welcome."

Morwen burst into tears. "Why, that is exactly what Salvis said to Petroc when we met him on High Hill! That really must have been a message from the King!"

The King had spoken to them! He was with them! They praised him until it seemed as though the roof of the farmhouse would be raised.

Martha stood before the assembly and lifted her hands. Her eyes were closed. Tears streamed down her cheeks.

"In good times I have praised the King! In my sadness I shall still praise the King, who shall reign over Karensa for evermore!"

Chapter 19

Where dolphins race with rainbows

Luke and Rosie lived on the farm all through the Time of Snows. These were days of fellowship and love, one for the other, as the sorrow they shared drew them close together and brought healing.

With the Guardians gone, life quickly returned to normal in the fisher village and on the surrounding farms. Morwen's family had many good friends, who made sacrifices to help them through the worst of their hardship.

They worked hard, and when the snow thawed, crops were sown to yield a late harvest.

During the cold days of the Time of Snows, Luke and Holly became firm friends, but Rosie was lonely. Her days were spent with Martha, who she loved dearly, but often Rosie would sit alone, her eyes sad and distant as she thought about Petroc. The farm was empty without him.

When the Time of New Birth brought blossom and wild flowers, Luke and Rosie had become like other young people on Karensa. Luke's fair hair now reached his shoulders. Rosie was resigned to having plaits. They were both healthy and strong and the farm flourished in Amos and Esram's hands.

During this time, neither Luke nor Rosie had any

thought of returning to Cornwall. They were content to stay here.

One day, just before the Time of Plenty, friends and neighbours gathered in the orchard behind the farm. The sun filtered through the branches of the apple trees. A warm breeze drifted across the fields. Birds sang. The air was fragrant with blossom and bumble bees hummed gently. The people spoke in hushed voices as they waited patiently for the special moment to arrive.

Esram, a tall young man with a gentle heart, stood with Luke. They were both dressed in new tunics of dark green. Esram seemed nervous.

Morwen, Rosie and Holly walked slowly from the farmhouse to the orchard. Morwen, now a lovely maiden of fifteen, was dressed in palest willow green. Her hair drifted around her shoulders in a red-gold cloud, crowned with a wreath of white flowers. Rosie and Holly walked behind, both in yellow and both with flowers in their hair.

Esram and Morwen faced each other. Esram spoke first. All nervousness gone, his voice was firm and steady.

"Morwen, before all our friends, I take you as my betrothed. I promise to always love you and care for you. In due time I promise to take you as my wife, and that will be the happiest day of my life. I make this promise before the assembly and before the King."

Now it was Morwen's turn. Her voice was not very loud, but it was strong and true.

"I thought when Petroc died I should never smile

again, but Esram, you have made it possible for me to be happy once more. I take you as my betrothed. I promise to love and respect you always, to be your wife, and mother to our children. I make this promise before the assembly and before the King."

Luke took Esram's hand and Rosie took Morwen's hand and they joined them together, making the couple handfast until the day they were old enough to be married. The guests sighed and then applauded loudly.

Luke looked at the girl with red hair who he had once hoped to make his own. Her face was radiant.

Rosie was crying, but these were tears of joy. Martha looked very proud, yet a little sad.

Morwen whispered to Esram, then she left his side and, taking Rosie's hand, led her across the farmyard to the place beneath the cherry tree where Petroc lay. Morwen removed the flowers from her hair and placed them on Petroc's grave.

"You were the best brother in the world," she said softly. "My sweet Petroc, be happy for me."

Rosie removed her own flowers and did the same.

"Petroc, you will always have a special place in my heart. I loved you so much. You were always true to the King and true to your friends, and... and you broke my heart when you died."

"Petroc will be happy for you, Morwen. I'm glad for you, too. You and Esram, you were meant to be." Luke had joined them and was giving them his blessing.

The three friends hugged each other. No more words were needed to express how they were feeling.

Later, while everyone was feasting and dancing, Rosie tugged at her brother's hand and led him outside. As they had done so many times before, they walked down to the farm gate.

"It'll soon be summer," Rosie observed.

"You mean the Time of Plenty."

For a little while they stood by the gate, looking at the Dark Forest, High Hill, the mist that never moved from the horizon. The sky was blue, white clouds drifting across from the sea.

"Karensa is waking up again, Luke. Lambs have been born. The days grow long and warm... Luke, I wonder how Pepper got on with the vet?"

Luke understood what she was saying.

"Yes," he replied. "Yes, Rosie, I believe it's time to go home."

"I think we should go to the Royal Palace," Rosie continued. "I want to be near Salvis for one last time."

Luke looked back at the farmhouse where the people they had grown to love were still celebrating.

"What about the others? We can't just go. Shouldn't we say goodbye?"

"No, they'll understand. Today, they'll hardly notice we're missing. When they do, they'll know we've gone home," Rosie said wisely.

"How do you know we can get home from the Royal Palace?"

"I don't. I just feel that's where we should go. I don't want to say goodbye, Luke. There have been too many goodbyes."

Luke saw the grave beneath the cherry tree. "Yes, there have been too many goodbyes."

Soon, they had crossed the Dark Forest and stood in the meadow. The Royal Palace shone in the sunlight. They were awed by its splendour. It was even more beautiful than they remembered, for now it was surrounded by an aura of gold.

In the distance they could just see the dark shadows of Bellum's castle, but this did not take any glory from the Palace of the King.

Rosie sighed. "It's so lovely! The first time I saw it, I thought it was a fairy castle. You laughed at me, Luke."

"We were much younger then," he said soberly. "I'm not laughing now."

"No," she agreed, "we're not laughing now."

"Do you really want to go home?"

Rosie nodded. "Part of me will be sad to go. I shall miss our friends and Martha and the farm... and Petroc... "

She looked so unhappy that Luke put his arms around her.

"Petroc's not here any more, Rosie." He pointed to the Royal Palace. "Look, that's where he is now! We can't go there."

Everything was suddenly too much for Rosie. "Oh Luke, I do want to go home. Let's ask Salvis to help us. Let's ask him right this minute!"

They called from the depth of their hearts. It seemed as though the farm, and High Hill and the fisher village and the Dark Forest, and all the places and the people they loved, gently faded into the mist. Only the Royal Palace remained.

Instead of fading away, the light from the Palace moved towards them and fell upon them, and for a brief moment they were able to see inside the Great

Hall, where the King's servants, dressed in white, sang praises before the Three Thrones. It was the most wonderful music, more beautiful than anything they had ever heard. They were not permitted to see the place where Salvis was enthroned because they were not able to look upon his glory. But they did see a tall young man with red hair.

Petroc turned his head towards them and smiled. In that smile was every moment they had shared and every word that had not been spoken.

Luke and Rosie clung tightly to each other, closing their eyes as the light from the Royal Palace covered them and showered them with love.

When they opened their eyes there was sand beneath their feet and they were on the beach at Poldawn. It had stopped raining. The mist over the sea had cleared.

"Your face!" Rosie exclaimed. "Luke, your face is bright like the sun!"

"So is yours! We've brought Karensa back with us!"

Even as they spoke, the light faded, but the radiance was still in their hearts.

"Luke... do you really think... I mean, Salvis... we know he's like Jesus, don't we? Only, he's on Karensa, not here. It's really hard to understand."

For possibly the first time ever, Luke had an answer for his sister.

"I don't think we should even try to understand. God only ever had one Son and that's Jesus. When we do wrong things, and we're sorry, God forgives us because of Jesus."

"It says that in the Bible. Once, we learnt this verse in Youth Church." She began to recite. "John, chapter three, verse sixteen...

'For God loved the world so much that he gave his only Son, so that everyone who believes in him may not die, but have eternal life.'

It was ages ago we learnt that, yet I still remember it."

"You've answered your own question with it," her brother replied. "Every time we've been to the island, it makes me want to know Jesus more and more. Everything that happened on Karensa, the Guardians, the meetings at the farm, and... and Petroc, have helped me make up my mind. When I leave school, I'm going to work for Jesus, big time!"

Rosie gave a cry of delight and pointed out to sea.

"Look! Two dolphins making rainbows in the sea, just like they used to in the Bay of Dolphins! Remember the song our mother used to sing about the island?"

"*Where sea birds fly from rocks of gold, and dolphins race with rainbows...* Every time I see a rainbow, I'll think of Karensa," he replied.

"Every time I see a rainbow, I'll remember Petroc," said Rosie, but her voice was not sad any more. "He looked so happy in the Royal Palace!"

"I know... Rosie... we believe Mum's now in heaven, just like Petroc's in the Royal Palace, don't we?"

"Of course we do."

"Well... Mum will be happy there, just like Petroc is so happy in the Palace."

Rosie nodded. She didn't trust herself to speak. Her sadness welled up suddenly, and without warning.

Luke had an idea. It was difficult for him to explain. Deep feelings were so much easier to share on Karensa than they were at home.

"Rosie, d'you know what I'd like to do? I know we've both asked Jesus into our lives, but I think we should do it again, as a sort of promise to serve Jesus from now on in a new way. I feel like... like I only want to do the things he's got planned for me. Nothing else matters."

Rosie felt like that too. So, as they watched the dolphins racing with rainbows, Luke said a prayer and Rosie repeated it with him.

"Lord Jesus, I'm really sorry for the wrong things I've done. Please forgive me. Thank you that you died on the cross to take away my sins so I can go to heaven. I know you love me, and I love you. Please be Lord of my life and be my friend for ever."

As they said that very special prayer, the wonderful love of Jesus stirred in their hearts.

They were still standing together when Stacey and Dad arrived with Pepper. The little collie was none the worse for her vaccination, and she raced across the beach to greet them. It was as though they had never been away.

Luke bent down and stroked the dog's silky ears. It was good to be home, but he knew that the real battle had only just begun. The silver serpent and

139

the golden sword were as real here as they had been on Karensa.

Life was about choices. There was a right way, the way of the golden sword. This meant trusting Jesus and staying true to God's Word in the Bible. And there was a wrong way, the way of the silver serpent which might seem attractive, but always led to unhappiness.

Petroc had made his choice. So had Morwen. So had Esram and Holly. So had Luke and Rosie.

Stacey was looking at them with a puzzled expression on her kind face.

"What have you two been up to? You look... I don't know, you look different."

"Better, or worse?" Rosie asked.

"Better," said Dad. "Definitely better."

The family linked arms, Dad and Stacey, Rosie and Luke, and, with Pepper running in front, they went home.

THE STORY OF THE GREAT KING WILL NEVER END

The earlier books in the Tales of Karensa *series...*

Where Dolphins race with Rainbows
Jean Cullop

"Welcome to Karensa."

Luke opened his eyes, blinking against the strong sunlight. He was sprawled on his back on soft, dry sand. In front of him the sea was calm and deepest blue, the waves lapping gently against the shore.

So the mist and the storm were a dream? He was safely back at Poldawn.

But as he struggled to sit up he realised that there had been no dream. This was not Poldawn. This was a bay of clean, flat sand surrounded by cliffs, lush with flowering plants and bushes unlike anything he had ever imagined. What was more, he was being watched by a group of the strangest looking people he had ever seen.

ISBN 1 85999 383 4

Castle of Shadows
Jean Cullop

The King gave a loud cry, a cry that resounded through the entire universe. "Now my Son who was dead is alive again! Now my people can come to me once more! Now, Salvis, you wear your royal robes... One day you will judge the people of Karensa and from now onward all those who trust in you will be welcomed into the Royal Palace. Meanwhile, let the battle continue. Now my people must choose whom they will follow and Bellum will try everything in his power to keep them from coming to me. My friends, this is where the real conflict starts."

Veritan lifted high the golden sword of truth and a great and mightly call to arms resounded around the Hall and was carried to the ends of the Earth.

ISBN 1 85999 463 6

Children of the Second Morning
Jean Cullop

Rosie hesitated by the wooden door. "Luke, think! If we go through there we may not be able to get back! At least not for ages. Remember last time. We were on Karensa for nearly a year. Think of the dangers, Luke! Think of sleeping on straw mattresses! Think of boring food and no telly, and work instead of school... and there are other dangers on Karensa. Think about Bellum!"

Luke closed his eyes, trying to make sense of his thoughts. Karensa was calling him. Salvis was calling him. It was like going home. The call on his life was strong and he couldn't deny it.

He felt Salvis close to them, so close that he could almost feel his great heart beating. Just to be there, on Karensa again... The call became stronger and stronger.

ISBN 1 85999 526 8